Praise for *Crazy Heart*

"A measure of Thomas Cobb's talent is t[...] [...]es story amusing even as we watch him fall. Bad is entirely sympathetic, and his crazy heart is vivid; the milieu is as resonant as a steel guitar, and the plot moves along without skipping a beat."

—*New York Times Book Review*

"*Crazy Heart* is a beautiful book. . . . The characters are cut cleanly out of America—the roadside West, the dance halls and beer joints, the occasional big concert, Houston, Nashville, Southern California, and the endless, eternal hotel rooms that are as close to home as a country singer ever gets. . . . Bad Blake is a man you will not soon forget."

—*Washington Times*

"[Cobb's] picture of the scraggly underside of Western music is brutally convincing."　　　　　　　　　　　　　　　　　　—*The New Yorker*

"Blake's dedication to, and integrity towards, his country music is more than matched by Cobb's moving, respectful evocation of the world of country music, and the life and times of Bad Blake."

—*Boston Herald*

"A masterpiece . . . [Cobb] has created an unforgettable character who engages not only your interest but your emotion . . . and who proceeds to take you on a roller-coaster ride through his tawdrily tumultuous life."

—*Chicago Tribune*

"Thomas Cobb has written a bitter, witty psychological profile of an aging genius that is also a wonderful celebration of country music. Bad Blake lives at the poor end of the rainbow, but you'll never forget him. *Crazy Heart* is a splendid achievement."　　　　—Donald Barthelme

About the Author

THOMAS COBB was born in Chicago, Illinois, and grew up in Tucson, Arizona. He is the author of the novel *Shavetail* and the short story collection *Acts of Contrition*. He lives in Rhode Island with his wife.

CRAZY HEART

Thomas Cobb

corsair

Constable & Robinson Ltd
3 The Lanchesters
162 Fulham Palace Road
London W6 9ER
www.constablerobinson.com

First published in the US in 1987 by HarperCollins Publishers

First published in the UK by Viking,
an imprint of Penguin Books Ltd, 1988

This UK edition published by Corsair,
an imprint of Constable & Robinson Ltd, 2010

A copy of the British Library Cataloguing in
Publication data is available from the British Library

ISBN: 978-1-84901-512-7

Printed and bound in the EU

1 3 5 7 9 10 8 6 4 2

For my mother and father

Chapter One

He's standing in the bowling alley parking lot in front of his 1978 Dodge van with burnt valves. He pulls his shirt away from his skin. Soaked, it sticks to him as fast as he pulls it away. Above him a sign announces: "Winter Leagues Now Forming." Below that it says, "Country Record Star / Bad Blake / Here / Friday, August 12."

He is trying to shake a dream. At a rest stop in New Mexico he dreamed he crouched before a low stone wall. Behind him was a man with a gun. On either side was one of his ex-wives. Bad understood they were to be shot, slaughtered like pigs. He wanted to run, but he could not decide whether to run or try to save one or both of the wives. He could not decide and he could not run. He remained crouched and waiting. He can still feel the pressure on the tendons in the backs of his legs.

He goes for his Pall Malls. The pack is nearly empty, loose and slick with sweat. He gets one lit and looks at the sign. A fucking bowling

3

alley, he thinks. They got you in a fucking bowling alley, right in the fucking middle of fucking nowhere Colorado. You should have known, you're old and fat, and now you are bowling alley material. Oh, Jack, he thinks, Jack, you bastard.

Inside, the bowling alley is full of light and the smell of wax. The air-conditioning hits hard and turns his soaked shirt icy. He is breathing fast, his heart pounding in shuffle time. He reaches for another cigarette, thinks better of it, and goes off to find the manager. A single bowler is working in the middle of thirty lanes. Bad hears the drop, the steady, straight tone of the roll, and waits for the impact. When it comes, it is a hollow thump like a drummer's wood block as the pins drop.

"Bad Blake!" the manager exclaims. "I'm proud to meet you. God, I used to listen to you when I was just a kid." Bad's heart thumps. He manages a wheeze and a smile and pumps the manager's hand.

"Have a good trip?" the manager wants to know.

"Long," Bad says. "Long but good. Played Clovis, New Mexico, last night. Saw some real pretty country. Glad to be here." Momentarily, he has forgotten where the hell he is.

The Spare Room is dark and quiet, though Bad can still hear the faint hiss and thump of the lone bowler. "Down there is the band stand," the manager explains. Bad notes the shadow of a drum kit and microphones on a raised platform. He heads for the bar. Among the bowling trophies and beer company gewgaws behind the bar, enormous fish swim back and forth in a lighted aquarium. Bad slides onto a barstool, careful of his hemorrhoids.

"Darlin'," he calls to the barmaid, "bring me a J.D. up, beer back." He smiles and points to the fish. "Buy one for the boys in the backroom there, too."

"Three twenty-five," she says when she brings his drinks. She is young and pretty in a sullen way. Bad winks. "On my tab, darlin'."

"No tab."

"I'm Bad Blake, little darlin'. I'm with the band. Hell, I am the band."

She turns and walks away. A minute later the manager is at Bad's side.

"Mr. Blake, we have a real nice room for you over in the Starlight Inn, and of course your meals are taken care of, but we can't let you run a bar tab. It's in the contract. Mr. Greene of Greene and Gold put that in himself."

4

Bad reaches out. For a second he is ready to grab the gristly knob of the manager's Adam's apple and crush it. Instead, he touches the man's shoulder and squeezes gently. "If you and Jack have an agreement, we'll all have to stick by it. Don't worry yourself about it, old buddy."

Jack, he thinks, you heifer-fucker, someday I will purely kill you. When I'm in your office you're on my leg; when I'm on the road, you're on my back.

"How much?" he asks the barmaid.

"Three twenty-five."

Bad looks hard at the shot. He's sweating. The cigarette between his fingers is wavering. His throat is raw from the Pall Malls. He wants the whiskey, but he has almost no cash left, and he knows he will want the drink even more later on. Still, right now he wants it more than he ever wanted any of his ex-wives. He digs four dollars from his pocket. When the barmaid brings back the change, he keeps it.

"Mr. Blake." The manager is back at his shoulder. "Let me personally offer you all the free bowling you want."

Bad nearly chokes. He swallows it, but the whiskey still burns in his nose.

"I just want you to know you're real welcome here."

"I can tell that, old buddy, I can tell."

In his room, Bad punches the air conditioner to "max." He hates air-conditioning, but he can't stop sweating. He strips off his soaked shirt and falls across the bed. He runs his hands across his broad belly and groans. Two orders of griddle cakes and sausage he ate in New Mexico have turned to pure, burning sulfur. The bedspread, some sort of cigarette-burned nylon over a thin foam-rubber backing, sticks to his skin. He longs for the old days and chenille bedspreads with zigzag patterns.

On the TV, a man and woman in fluorescent colors embrace. When they part, their lips move but no sound comes out. Bad considers getting up to turn up the sound, but decides it's good enough this way. The couple, he supposes, is talking about what a prick Jack Greene is. He doesn't want to find out any different.

Bad is in the back of his old Silver Eagle touring bus, almost asleep, listening to the bus's wheels on the blacktop, a sound like the softest set of brushes he has ever heard. He loves the sound even more than he loves silence after a night of playing. He calls to Marge and gets no answer. Then he calls Suzi, though he was married to her years after Marge. There is still no answer. He gets out of the bunk and heads for the front of the bus. He wants to know where he is and who he is married to. "Tommy," he calls, but Tommy Sweet doesn't answer. Everyone on the bus is asleep and he cannot wake them. The bus driver is his father, and he can't wake him, either. He returns to the back of the bus.

Bad's heart lurches as though it is coming loose from its moorings. He blinks and groans. Despite the air-conditioning, he is still covered with sweat. The hair on his chest and belly, sweated flat, radiates like a thousand needles from his heart. On the television, a woman throws up her hands in joy as a flock of bluebirds flies from her washing machine. The birds have, he hopes, just crapped all over her clean clothes. He gets up and takes his damp shirt into the bathroom to wash it out in the sink.

"Mr. Greene is still on the other line, Mr. Blake."

"I'll wait, darlin'."

The highlight of this evening looks to be dinner in a restaurant with thin redwood paneling and ferns that drip down to the salad bar.

"Darlin', you ever been in Pueblo, Colorado?"

"I don't believe so, Mr. Blake."

"Well, I wish you were here right now, Sweetness, because you'd sure as hell be the best thing Pueblo ever had to offer."

When she laughs, Bad sees an image of Brenda walking across the plush carpet of Jack's office, bringing him a cup of coffee to take the edge off his embarrassment as Jack makes him wait. He hears the shush of her stockings under her tight skirt.

"Matter of fact, Brenda, I really wish you were here tonight, because I just might be the best thing that Pueblo, Colorado, has to offer."

Her laugh is efficient. "Here's Mr. Greene."

"Bad, how's Arizona?"

"Colorado."

"Right, Colorado. So, how's Colorado?"

"You ever seen Colorado?"

"Yeah, years ago."

"It's still here. Listen, Jack, I got some problems."

6

"O.K., what can I do?"

"Jack, last night I got a call from Suzi."

"How the hell did she find you?"

"I was going to ask you that, but obviously you don't know where the hell I am."

"Jesus, Bad. I got six acts on the road right now, including a rock group that just trashed a Ramada Inn in Memphis. I get confused, O.K.? Now, which one's Suzi?"

"Four. The little brunette. The one that whines."

"Oh, right. She was a doll, Bad."

"I can't stand whiners."

"Then why the hell did you marry her?"

"I thought she'd stop whining if I did. Jack, she says she hasn't gotten a check in quite a bit. She's whining again."

"Right. Well, receipts are a little slow coming in off this trip. I guess they still use Pony Express out there."

"But there are royalties."

"Yeah, but . . . Oh hell, Bad, I didn't want to tell you until you came in off this swing. J.M.I. cut out *So Sweet, So Bad.*"

"Jack, that fucker was still selling."

"It had slowed, slowed a lot, and Tommy's got nine albums right now and a new one next month. That's a lot of product to rack and the chains don't like crowding."

"Fuck the chains. The chains have got less brains than I got ex-wives."

"Them and most of the world, Bad."

"What about Tommy, what about the new album? I'll be off the road in a couple of weeks. I can go straight to L.A. or Nashville. We can get right to work on it."

"Tommy wants to know if you've got new material."

Bad is looking at a cardboard painting above the television set, sailboats on a stormy sea. The colors are streaked and blotchy—red, blue and white against black and gray. He can't figure why anyone would want to look at such a mess, much less paint it.

"You know I don't have new material," he says. "Hell, I'm not new material. There's nothing wrong with the old stuff. We did real well with it the last time out. A hell of a lot better than he did with his goddamned gunfighter albums."

"Tommy thinks he's leaning too hard on the old stuff. He doesn't want people to think he's riding the gravy train."

"That son-of-a-bitch has a lifetime pass on the gravy train."

7

"Come on, Bad. Remember who's asking who to do a record here."

"Jack, you jerk-off. You get out here in, in, Clovis, goddamned, New Mexico, or Pueblo, kiss-my-ass, Colorado, and you play in a piano bar or a bowling alley, backed by a bunch of old bastards with brush cuts and string ties. You look out on a bar full of blue-hairs who've checked their teeth at the door. You smile and sweat and sing 'Slow Boat' three times a night. You get up the next fucking morning at five o'clock and drive three hundred miles with piles so bad it feels like you've got a nest of fire ants up your ass, and then you tell me about riding the goddamned gravy train. You and Tommy Sweet both try it sometime."

"Bad, Bad. Calm down. Tommy says he wants new material. I'll keep talking, but he's holding the cards. You know that, I know it, and Tommy Sweet sure as hell knows it."

"You keep talking, Jack. And you tell Tommy for me that he wouldn't know country music if it came up and kicked him in his world-famous ass. And tell him that one of these days, it sure as hell is going to."

Jack keeps talking, and Bad puts the phone against his belly and looks back at the painting above the television.

"Jack, is it true they've taught monkeys how to paint?"

"What? What the hell are you talking about? Monkeys?"

"Jack, I'm broke. I need money."

"I sent you money when you were still in Texas. I sent you plenty."

"Wasn't enough, old buddy, I need more."

"Bad, if I send you money, you'll go on one of your famous benders and wind up back here, who knows when, sick, broke and married."

"I ain't going to marry anybody."

"Look, you're going to build a nice piece of change out there on the road. Even when your exes get their cut, you'll have a little left over for once. I'm going to make sure you keep it for a little while."

"I'm down to my last ten bucks."

"That will get you to Santa Fe. You've got cards for gas, and you've got expenses all the way. You'll be there soon. I'll have some cash waiting in Santa Fe."

"Jack, I'm fifty-six years old and I only have ten bucks."

"Spend it wisely, Bad."

"Jack, did I ever tell you that your mother used to bite when she gave head?"

"I love you, too. Bye-bye."

Bad hangs up the phone and rolls over onto his back. Why the hell would someone want to paint a streaky, piddling-ass little picture like that that didn't mean jack-shit to anyone?

In the liquor store, Bad lusts for the short, square bottle of Jack Daniel's. He stoops to the pint bottle of Heaven Hill and something drops down his back. He wears an old shirt that Nudie himself designed. It is full of beadwork, but the thread is rotting and beads drip down his back into his pants.

"Mr. Blake?"

When he stands, beads fall through his pants and into his boots. His heart stutters.

"Goddamn. It is you. It really is Bad Blake right here in my store." A short, balding man reaches out his hand. "I'm Bill Wilson. I'm a big fan, and just real pleased to meet you."

Bad smiles and looks back to the cheap bourbon.

"Here. Here, Mr. Blake. Here's the Jack Daniel's." Bill Wilson pulls a full liter of J.D. from the shelf. "Being in the business and a big fan and all, I kind of keep track of what the stars drink. It's kind of a hobby, you know. Willie Nelson and his Lone Star Beer, Haggard and his George Dickel, Tommy Sweet and his Southern Comfort, and Bad Blake and his Jack Daniel's. Of course, I never thought I'd actually have a star right here in my store."

Bad eyes the bottle in Bill Wilson's hand and wheezes with desire.

"My wife Barbara is one of your biggest fans. She'll flat die when she finds out you were here in the store. She's out getting her hair done right this minute. We're going to your show tonight. I think she's having it done just for you. Of course"—he winks—"I expect to get the real benefit of it. But if you could sing 'Slow Boat' for her tonight, it would sure mean the world to her. It might"—he winks again—"mean a lot to me, too."

"You got it, old buddy. You sure got it." Bad can't take his eyes off that bottle of Jack Daniel's. " 'Slow Boat' for Barbara. You got it."

"She'll be thrilled. She really will," Bill Wilson says. "And here, take this. I want to be able to tell everyone that I bought Bad Blake a drink."

Out in the sunlight, Bad looks at the bottle and then up to the sky. Sweet Baby Jesus, thank you.

A fighter plane trails white across a turquoise sky. Bad is already a quarter finished with the bottle when someone pounds on his door. He gets up, puts on the Nudie shirt. More beads drip down his back.

At the door is a young man with long hair and a wispy beard. "Hi. I'm Tony." Bad blinks in incomprehension.

"Tony," the young man insists. "Tony and the Renegades. Your band."

Of course. Bad nods. The backup band. His backup bands on the road are always of two types: young rock-and-rollers or old men who have been playing his songs for years without getting them right. He supposes that if he got to choose, he would take the kids.

"Me and the boys, we're over at the alley, setting up. We were wondering what time to start rehearsing."

"Soon as you can. Start rehearsing as soon as you can and do it often as you can. That's the secret. You can't rehearse enough."

"What I mean is, what time are you coming to rehearsal?"

Bad sighs and takes Tony by the arm and leads him out to the van. "I got lead sheets if you all can read music, chord charts if you can't. I got cassettes and a play list. You go on. I'll be by later. I already done my rehearsing."

Bad turns back to the room and the bottle. Tony follows. "Mr. Blake, it would mean a lot to us if you would come on over early. I mean, we need to get the leads down and all that."

"Leads?" Bad asks. "Leads? Son," he asks seriously, "are they paying you more than they're paying me?"

"But," Tony goes on, "I thought you could show us some things, teach us some of that old stuff Bad's Boys used to do. Is it true you taught Tommy Sweet how to play guitar?"

Bad ignores the remark about Tommy. "All right," he says. "You all go listen to the cassettes. Listen carefully. Study the lead sheets. Give me an hour to get some dinner and then I'll be over." Bad doesn't know what he can teach them. He has learned only two things as a musician he could ever put into words: keep your wrist steady, and don't ever marry nobody.

Bad pokes at the chicken-fried steak. Pale gravy oozes from it. Next to the chicken-fried steak is a scoop of mashed potatoes and a spoonful of corn. Road food. Road food is always neutral in color and taste. It only turns exciting a couple of hours later. He has learned to eat early and not make rude noises onstage.

The hostess-cashier slides into the booth across the table from him. She exhales a long stream of cigarette smoke over his food. "Everything O.K.?"

"Fine." Bad nods. "Just fine."

She wears her black hair pinned in curls on top of her head, and her makeup thick. When she winks at him, a small knot of mascara sticks to her lower lash. She wears a red nylon blouse and a plastic name tag that says, "Howdy, I'm Jo Ann." "Mind if I smoke?" she asks. Bad waves his hand.

"This is the time of day I hate," she says. "Waiting for the rush to start. It's O.K. once it does, and after it's over, but thinking about it, my God, I hate that. You must like to eat early and avoid the crowds. Be able to eat in peace without a bunch of people asking for autographs and stuff. Mind if I ask you a question?"

"Shoot."

She reaches over and taps his knuckle with a long red fingernail. "I always wondered if you had a good time singing those songs. Because, God, I hope to tell you, I had me a couple of real good times listening to them." Her laugh is deep and a little raspy from the cigarette smoke. "Of course, I've had a couple of rotten ones, too, come to think of it."

"So have I, darlin', so have I. Anything you want to hear tonight?"

She bites her tongue as she thinks. Her teeth are stained red from the lipstick. "You do anything from that album you do with Tommy Sweet?"

"A few. The standards. 'Faded Love,' 'Please Release Me,' 'Crazy Arms.'"

"Any of those. God, I just love that album. *Memories: So Sweet, So Bad.* Of course, I love Tommy Sweet, too."

"So does Tommy, darlin'."

When she laughs the raspy laugh, she reminds him of his ex-wife, Marge. He likes her.

"You two don't get along anymore?"

Bad shrugs. "What the wives didn't get off that album, Tommy did."

Jo Ann gets embarrassed, then flirty. She runs her finger up his forearm. "Why don't you tell me your real name?"

"You want to know that, you got to marry me, darlin'. That's why so many have. Otherwise, it's just Bad. I was Bad long 'fore any niggers thought to be."

Bad pushes through the door and into The Spare Room. Rock music swells up and staggers him. He moves toward the bandstand,

11

carrying his guitar and amp. Tony and the Renegades stop as they see him approach, though the drummer continues to pound for a few more beats.

"I hope to God that wasn't one of my songs you were playing."

Tony steps down from the bandstand. "Mr. Blake, these are the Renegades." He runs through a list of names that Bad doesn't attempt to catch. The best thing about backup bands is that they are so easy to forget.

"That's it?" someone asks. "That's your equipment?"

"This," Bad says, unsnapping the case, "is a Gretsch Country Gentleman. A Country Gentleman with gold plate from the head to the tailpiece and an action that would put a twenty-year-old whore to shame." He looks at their stacked Marshall amps. "You fellows must go on the road a lot with those. Fun to tote. If you are playing loud enough to drown out this Roland Cube, you are playing way, fucking, too loud."

They take the play list in order. Bad relaxes into an easy set, just chording through the songs, playing simple verse-form leads at the breaks. Twice, he misses notes and wishes he had left just a little more of the Jack Daniel's in the bottle.

"Do some of that Tommy Sweet stuff for us," Tony insists.

There is no Tommy Sweet stuff. There is only Bad Blake stuff that Tommy Sweet has taken for his own. But he doesn't feel any need or use in explaining this right now. In "Slow Boat" he obliges them, running through a break full of hammers and pulls, the style he taught Tommy and that has become Tommy's signature.

"I don't know," Tony says. "I think Tommy plays it more like this." He begins the song again, throwing in double and triple pulls, trilling the high notes. "I think," he says, "that's more the sort of thing he does now. That's the way we like to play it."

"Keep working on that," Bad advises. "Someday Tommy will be playing this very same bowling alley. You all will still be here. You can show him. He'll like it. You can buy each other drinks. You can get drunk and be a couple of guitar-picking wonders together."

There are two hours before the show. Bad is watching television, still without sound. He is trying to get his heart to stop pounding. On the television, men in work clothes are yelling at a man in a suit. Bad takes a long pull at his bottle of Jack Daniel's. The man in the suit is unflappable and continues to smile. A young man in a mustache and

12

a Beech-Nut cap is yelling so hard Bad can see spit fly from his mouth. The man in the suit smiles and nods patiently, pretending he understands rage. The young man seems to be strangling on his. Bad likes the young man. Kill the fucker, he thinks. He takes another long pull on the bottle.

Bad is ready to get off the bus. He is wearing his red suit with the white lightning stripe up the pants leg. They are in the new town, and Bad is ready to do the new song. This is very important. But the young man in the Beech-Nut cap won't let him off the bus. He is screaming but there is no sound. The young man does not want Bad here. He doesn't like Bad's suit. He wants to know where Bad was fifteen years ago. Fifteen years ago, Bad wants to explain, he had to give concerts and make records, get married, divorced and married again. But right now, he has this new song, and if he can just sing it once, everything will be all right. The young man hates Bad's song and his suit. He is screaming so hard he showers Bad with spit. My God, Bad thinks, his spit will hit the lightning stripes on this yellow suit, and I will die.

Bad struggles across the parking lot of the bowling alley, carrying his guitar in one hand and the Roland Cube in the other. He is luminous in orange and white. He tries not to think of himself, an old fat man dressed in an orange suit with a white lightning stripe up each leg, white hat and white boots, and a heart doing the bump and grind.

At the back door, Tony and the Renegades are lounging, cooling off between sets. They watch Bad lurch across the parking lot. No one offers help.

"Hey," Tony calls at last, "it's showtime."

Bad pulls up even with Tony. He is wheezing hard and can feel the sweat dripping from under the band of his hat. The air is sharp with marijuana and Bad watches a joint go from hand to hand.

"We were afraid you weren't going to show."

The band members look at each other, smiling.

"Son, I have played sick, hurt, drunk, married, divorced, on the run, and run to the ground. Bad Blake has never pulled a no-show in his whole goddamned life. Not even in a fucking bowling alley, backed by a band of hippies." He takes the joint as it moves near him and pulls a long drag. He lets the smoke out and takes another deep drag.

"Better watch that stuff," Tony says. "Maui Wowie."

Bad looks at the joint and takes one more drag. "You sure they're not paying you more than they're paying me?"

The bar and bandstand are dark, and Bad stumbles on the riser. He unpacks the guitar, plugs in, adjusts the volume and waits for a note from Tony. He gets an A flat.

"Bring it up a half step."

"I'm in tune," Tony says. "I got an electronic tuning meter. I'm on."

"I got a fifty-six-year-old ear says you're off. Bring it up a half step."

When the band has retuned, Tony steps on the light switch and a single light brings up the microphone. The band moves into "Wild-wood Flower," uptempo, but rushed just a little. Back behind the amps, Bad tries to turn up loud enough to slow them down. He can't and speeds to catch up to them.

At the end of the first chorus, Tony moves up to the microphone and says, "Ladies and gentlemen, The Spare Room is proud to present country recording star 'The Wrangler of Love,' Mr. Bad Blake."

Bad steps forward to where the light is supposed to be turned on, but misjudges, and only his guitar neck and left hand are in the spot. He takes a sidestep into the light and swings into his jazzy instrumental, a simple melody, but quick and light, full of triplets that sound harder to play than they really are. Applause from the bar covers a couple of clinkers.

They move through the set as they have rehearsed, but still a little fast. Between "Love Came and Got Me" and "Faded Love," he tells the drummer to slow it down. It does no good. His throat feels full and tight, despite the Jack Daniel's he has been drinking all night. After "Faded Love" he ducks behind the amps and takes a pull from the bottle.

Back at the microphone, he tunes his slipping E string while he talks to the audience. "Thank you all, so much. I can't tell you how good it is to be here in Pueblo, Colorado. I've been all over the country, and I've found it's filled with good people. I want to tell you, a lot of them are right here in Pueblo." While the bar applauds, he turns and gives Tony the A. Tony returns it, in tune. "You know, one thing I've learned over the years is that if you don't give the folks what they want, they won't want anything from you again. I believe a few of you want to hear this next song. I had a hit on it about twenty years ago, when I was, let me see, just seven years old." He starts "Slow Boat" with the signature shift from A to D-flat minor to D and back to A.

The applause starts again. "This song is for all of you who have been so good to me for a long, long time now, but I also want to send it out special to a couple of my dear friends, Bill and Barbara. God, I think the world of them."

The band comes in behind him and forms a pocket for Bad to fit the melody into. Bill Wilson and Barbara, in matching shirts, jeans and boots, move out onto the floor. Barbara is a handsome woman, young and strong-looking. She is a full head taller than Bill. Bill, Bad figures, must be one capable son-of-a-bitch. Barbara leans her head down on Bill's, and they begin to turn across the dance floor. Bill beams. You may not be able to sell out a concert anymore, or cut a hit record, Bad thinks, but by God, you can still jerk them around.

When the song is over, Bad walks back behind the amps and takes another long pull at the bottle. Back at the microphone, the whiskey starts to push back up his throat. Tony starts "Please Release Me," and as Bad comes in behind him, he feels a flush of cold pass through his body. He intends to sing the song the way Lefty always did, bending the notes, taking them up and suddenly dropping them, but the first time he tries that full octave drop on "go," the whiskey comes up again. He fights it down, but loses the next two bars before he is able to open his mouth again. He starts low, and keeps it there, half a key below what the band is playing.

When he finally drags the song to a close, he says, "I'm awful sorry about that, folks. I've got me a frog in my throat that just don't want to behave. I believe I'll take a quick break and see if I can't send him back where he belongs. Tony and the boys here will do a couple of songs and then I'll be right back. We've got a long time and a lot of good songs we want to do for you yet."

As he moves away from the microphone, unplugging his guitar, he stumbles, and lands on one knee on top of his Roland Cube. When he looks up, all he can see is a red amplifier light, pulsing in the dark like the neon red heart of Jesus.

The next sensation he is aware of is a ridge of cold metal in his hand. He is outside the back door of the alley, on his knees, holding the rim of a garbage can. He pulls himself up and looks at the sky, a wash of stars. He is cold and shivering. He wipes his face with a handkerchief, then checks to see if he's kept his suit clean. It is

15

soaked with sweat. He bends down, picks up his hat and brushes at a streak of dirt that smears across the crown. He leans against the building and looks up. Stars spin slowly, but when he looks down he can focus and hold his field of vision. He coughs once and finds his throat clear.

Tony and the Renegades are just finishing some two-step he's heard on the radio when he climbs back up on the riser and begins the applause for the band.

He is shaky for the next two numbers. His voice wavers, and his playing is mechanical. He concentrates on staying on tempo with the band. They are still playing too fast, but it is easier to accept the tempo than to fight it. The band is getting edgy, bored with the steady progression of chords in the simplified play list. On "Cold, Cold Heart" Tony cuts in on him in the break and takes over the lead himself. Bad falls back into the rhythm pattern behind him.

By the time they are to the end of the play list, Tony has established a pattern of taking the leads. He plays verse form, full of the trills and pulls that he played in rehearsal. Bad's voice has steadied, but his hands are still cold and sweaty. He moves up to the microphone. "I've had a special request for this next song. Old Ray Price did it first, but I did it a couple years ago with a friend of mine." The bar starts to applaud. "Now, Tommy can't be with me tonight, but I want to do our version of this song, and send it out to Jo Ann, bless her pretty little heart."

He begins "Crazy Arms" chording the rhythm part, but determined to do his own lead. Between chorus and verse he plays a bridge of pedal-steel licks, playing three notes, bending the third while playing the other two straight. Dancers swing across the floor, including, he notices, Jo Ann on the arm of a tall, angular man with a high-crowned hat.

At the second chorus, he starts the pedal-steel licks again, intending to build a break based on them, connected by hammered runs. By now, Tony has caught on to the structure of the break and begins to play the melody line an octave higher. The result is a fine break, but it is Tony's lead, though Bad has created it. At the end of the song, Bad invites Tony to introduce the band. Tony finishes by introducing himself as lead guitar.

The last song is "It's Strange." The last couples take the dance floor. Bad has the lead, but he feels Tony crowding behind him, waiting for a chance to move in. The band's attention has revived, and

16

they are playing tight and purposefully for the first time all night. At the break, Bad takes a simple lead, adding in the hammers and pulls he used at rehearsal. When he reaches the end of the verse, Tony picks up the lead and plays it back, adding a blues riff at the end.

Bad accepts the riff and expands on it, remembering nights spent on Maxwell Street in Chicago, listening to the blues in the tight, packed clubs, the smell of smoke and sweat, and deep into the night, the nearly manic playing of bluesmen, entranced and glistening with sweat, picking up each other's leads, expanding and elaborating on them as he sat as close to the little bandstands as he could get, studying the technique, the intensity of some of the best players he had ever heard. He bends strings, first one note and then two. He runs a scale up the neck and then slides back down, making the guitar cry. He creates a shell of sound and climbs in and finds room to breathe. The dancing couples stop, stand and watch.

Tony starts to pick up the blues lead, falters on one note, then two. He swings uptempo, moving across the line between blues and rock, into his own territory. Bad catches the direction of the riff, finds the tempo and moves in on Tony. He takes the rock riff for a couple of bars and then adjusts his pickup controls and jerks hard on the tremolo bar. The big guitar shrieks. Bad rips through scales and lets the guitar feed back. Sweat pours from his head and splashes on the guitar. His heart pounds. He does not know what he is playing, but he keeps going, sure he will find his way through this. The guitar understands rage. Bad alternates chords and single-string leads. Tony stops and backs up a step. Bad finds an opening and begins a run, moving easily up the neck, keeping the tempo, but working his way back, winding down the furious tone of the song until he finds the spot he is looking for and moves into a quick, delicate reprise of the melody, playing triplets like a mandolin player.

He looks over to Tony and arches an eyebrow. Tony shakes his head and Bad accepts. "Ladies and gentlemen, it's been wonderful with you tonight. You all drive safely now, and the Lord willing, we'll get together again real soon. Good night."

As they settle into one last chorus, Bad shifts the key down a half step so he can end up in basso profundo. Tony steps to the microphone. "Ladies and gentlemen, the star of the show. Let's hear it for the great Bad Blake." He lets go of his guitar and leads the applause. Bad plays a quick riff and steps back as Tony cuts the stage lights.

*　　　*　　　*

Light is just starting to come through the window next to the bed. He has slept for a couple of hours without dreams. He is not sure what this means, but his heart has stopped pounding and his head is clear.

Jo Ann is still asleep. Her makeup has worn off, and her hair is tangled around her hand. She looks older, a little drawn, but Bad has always loved them, all of them, best this way. He dresses quietly and carries the white boots and hat in his hand. He waits until he is outside and pisses behind the open door of the van. He figures he has a couple of hours before the sweating starts again.

Chapter
Two

By the time the sun is full in the sky, he is starting to climb the hills. He is, he figures, another hour away from New Mexico. Along the side of the road the scrub brush has begun to turn to trees, and Colorado looks more like what he remembers from years earlier. He thinks about last night. He has played drunk before, drunk, sick drunk and stoned. But he has never let go that far in front of a bunch of kids. There is a certain pleasure in taking the boy to school, in showing him just how much he doesn't know about the instrument, but that sort of thing shouldn't be necessary. He shouldn't have to prove himself to a twenty-year-old.

Still, it has been a long time since he has played like that, and it feels good to get in and cut. There is a quick progression he played last night, just the smallest snatch of a melody, no more than four bars, that he still hears this morning. He hums it to himself, seeing if there is anything he can connect it to.

He is getting hungry. He still has only ten dollars and two hundred miles to Las Vegas, New Mexico. The melodic phrase keeps coming back to him, but he doesn't find the note that will carry it anywhere that seems to interest him. How much of his life has he spent just this way, tinkering with a few notes, looking for the next one in the series, looking for the one that will lead him to find the whole from the piece?

God bless credit cards.

A skinny boy with snaggled teeth takes Bad's card and runs it through the machine that stamps his Texaco number on the receipt. It is one hell of a thing when fifty-six-year-old men are sent out on the road with only ten dollars.

"Just the gas?" the boy asks.

"Can I put anything else on the card?"

"Hell, anything I got in here, except beer." He gestures around the inside of the station, which looks more like a damned grocery store than a gas station.

Bad walks down the aisles. Nothing here looks like breakfast. Still, breakfast costs cash. He takes two ham sandwiches, three hard-boiled eggs, a bag of potato chips, three fried peach pies, a handful of Milky Ways, a six-pack of Coke, a carton of Pall Malls, a *Playboy* magazine, and a red-and-yellow plastic lighter that says "Land of Enchantment."

"I got tires and batteries outside," the boy says.

"I believe this is all the hungry I got."

"I mean for your car."

"It ain't hungry at all."

The boy rings it up. Forty-seven eighty-three with the gas. Bad signs the receipt "B. Blake / Greene and Gold Productions."

"You must be on your way to the races," the boy says as he hands Bad the receipt.

"Races?"

"Yeah. You look like a horseman and all. I figured you was on your way to the races."

"Where?"

"Raton. About ten miles south. People have been coming through all week for the races. They run every day, all month long."

"Ten miles. And how far is, what the hell, Las Vegas?"

"Which one?"

"The one on this road—New Mexico."

"Well, the other one is on this road, too, if you're starting on this road. Of course, you'd have to get off it to get there."

22

"Las Vegas, New Mexico?"

"About a hundred and fifty miles, straight south."

Life has a way of dropping itself into your lap. He is down to his last ten bucks, but he has five and a half hours to make one hundred and fifty miles, and ten miles away there is a racetrack.

He leans on the rail, squinting at the racing form. He has bet two races, and he is two dollars and thirty cents to the good after expenses. He has paid two dollars to park, one dollar to get in, and fifty cents for a racing form. He is making old-lady bets and they are bringing him back. He bets two dollars on the favorite to show. One horse pays two thirty, and the other, which really does run third, pays four fifty.

"Don't believe that thing," an old guy in a straw hat and blue jeans tells him. "Those damn things don't tell the whole story. If they did, you can damn well bet you they wouldn't be selling them for no damn fifty cents."

"It's what I got."

"And you ain't got much there, let me tell you. Damn things don't tell the whole story."

"I don't ever expect the whole story. Except in dirty books."

"And you don't get it there, either. When's the last time some old gal farted in one of them books? You want the whole story, you got to find someone that knows it. Then you got to make sure he knows it. Then you got to convince him to tell you."

"You got someone who knows?"

"Hell, I ain't got nobody. I had me an old woman a while back, but she didn't want me sniffin' after nothing but her." The old guy hacks up a wad of phlegm and puts it over the rail and into the grass. "I sent her packing. I can't be roped down like that."

"Yeah. Well, there's that." Bad goes back to the racing form.

"What I got is myself. Myself is what I trust. And I know a couple things about ponies."

"I'm only betting this race. I got to get back on the road."

"I could use one of those cigarettes you got."

Bad shakes one out of the pack and lights it for him. The old guy doubles over with a fit of coughing. "Shit," he says. "I ain't got no lungs no more. What is this?" He looks at the cigarette. "Hell. Used to be, I thought only little girls smoked these things. I rolled my own out of Mexican tobacco. Now I ain't got no lungs. Ain't got no knees and I ain't got no lungs. I still got a brain, though. And"—he pokes

Bad in the ribs—"I still got me a pecker if you got some old gal who's got the hungries." He wheezes and hacks more phlegm. "I can tell you a goddamned thing or two about these nags here, too. Which one you figuring on?"

"Six."

"Old Judy's Pride. He can run. That form there will tell you that. Of course, that ain't the whole story."

"I kind of figured it might not be."

"Shit. You figure I'm jerking you. Hell, you ask anybody around here if old Shorty jerks people. Shit, no. Son-of-a-bitch. I know these goddamned horses. I help folks out. You're figuring on betting on Judy's Pride. You need helping out. That's all I'm trying to do. Let me explain one damned thing to you. Judy's Pride is skittish as hell. If he gets pushed into the rail, he's going to back off. There's an old boy riding this race that'll push him right through the fucking rail if he gets half a chance. That horse is going to finish out of the money, and your money is going to be about three steps behind him."

"What do you recommend?"

"Well, I was you, I'd get me a bottle of good whiskey and just set here and watch 'em run while the jackasses with the racing forms throw their money at 'em. That'd be a hell of a lot cheaper than the way you're going at it."

"I got to hit one more before I leave. And that number six looks good to me."

The old guy coughs again. "Hell. I got time invested in you. I tell you what. I'll give you the damn horse. You win, you slip me a fin. You lose, it don't cost you a dime other than the money you was all set to lose anyway."

Jesus. Bad wonders if everyone in Judah, Indiana, raises the kind of fools his mother did. "O.K. What do you have?"

"Stick Shift," the old boy says. "Stick Shift to win."

Bad goes back to the form. "Stick Shift hasn't run better than third in a single start."

"That's right. Twenty to one right now. Let me tell you something. That horse started the season with a bad knee. I watched him run this morning. He's ready, and he's got Jesse Castenada on top. That old boy will bring him in. He'll go after the six horse on the rail, and he'll take the rail the rest of the way in. He's healthy. Six is the only one that can flat outrun him, and old Jesse Castenada will make sure he doesn't. That boy is as smart as he is mean. And he's meaner than day-old coffee."

What the hell, Bad figures. He's only got twelve dollars. If he loses five, what the damn difference does it make? The old guy has him too confused to figure anything out for himself anyway. "Let's go to the window," he says. The old guy gimps along behind him.

When Bad has his five dollars down, they head back around the grandstand for the race. "Why don't you bet if you know so much?"

The old guy looks at him. "I suspect you done some drinking in your time."

"Yeah. A bit."

"A bit, my ass. You know what I'm talking about. Betting's gambling. Drinking's too damn serious for gambling. I pick a few horses, I make a few bucks. I never worry about a damn dry streak. I get me a bottle and a place to drink it, what the hell do I need money for?"

When the horses leave the gate, number six takes the early lead, and Stick Shift hangs well back in the pack. Around the far turn, Stick Shift moves up, and they run neck and neck until the last turn, when Stick Shift moves up by a neck and crowds toward the rail. It is just as the old guy has said it would be. Coming out of the final turn, it is Stick Shift on the rail. Judy's Pride has fallen back a full length, and Stick Shift has the rail and only space to the finish line.

Stick Shift has come off at seventeen to one. At the window, Bad collects eighty-five dollars. He gives the old guy a twenty.

"Thanks. I'm obliged. I only need five."

"Buy yourself a good bottle. Have a good time."

"Hell, I'll damn well do that. Someday, someone will do you a favor. Hell, I'll probably be dead by then, but someone will do you one. And I'm going to goddamn hope you don't need it too bad."

He has started the first set feeling good. Things have turned around. He can sense that things are going to go his way for a while. Now, deep into the set, he is getting weary, trying to sing half a beat slower to find the band's pace. When he slows, they slow further. He's afraid the whole set is going to wind down like a four-dollar watch. He has taken to giving the drummer the beat before each song. He counts it, the drummer taps it. When Bad turns his back, the drummer slips right back to the slower tempo.

"That was 'Cold, Cold Heart,'" he says. "Hank Williams did that. He's dead now. Next we're going to do Lefty Frizzell's 'Please Release Me.' Lefty's dead, too. All this done by a singer who's nearly dead. Backed by the band that probably killed them all." And damned if the band doesn't take a bow.

He lets the band take the tempo and tries to adjust to it. Instead of singing the song in the lower register, letting it rumble, he decides to try it Lefty's way, bending the notes. That way, he figures, he can get a little ahead of the band, and bend the notes until they come strangling up behind him. It works better than anything else he has tried. He's not Lefty, but then neither are all the singers who are trying to imitate him, and the people in the audience who don't remember Lefty know the imitators and appreciate the sound.

At the break, he stays at the bar. He has two quick whiskeys, then switches to Coca-Cola. The memory of last night is still fresh, and if he is going to do one more set dragging this band behind him, he's going to have to stay sober.

He shakes hands and smiles. "Of course," he says. "How the hell are you doing?" "Des Moines, sixty-two—hell yes, I remember. We had a fine time." "It's good to see you again." "It's real nice to meet you." "You take care of yourself now." "Sure I'll play 'Slow Boat' again for you." "Tommy's in Nashville, working on a new album. Next time I see him, I'll say 'hey' for you." People are pressing notes written on cocktail napkins into his hands while he talks. He pockets them. Most of them are requests for dedications of "Slow Boat."

While he shakes hands and talks, he looks around the bar. It is full of wood paneling and cowboy art. From the wall opposite him, a deer stares at him with black marble eyes. It is a huge buck that must have run and rutted through the mountains for years until some accountant or bricklayer with a pickup truck, a five-hundred-dollar rifle and a case of jolting bad desire slammed him into the rocks. Someone has put a baseball cap on its head, between the magnificent rack. Bad takes out his glasses and looks.

"Let's fuck," it says on the cap. Jesus, isn't that just the way? As if it isn't bad enough that they run you to the ground sooner or later, they insist on making you into a fool.

"Bad?" A tall, thin man in a western shirt reaches a hand to him. "It's good to see you again, Bad."

"Hell, old buddy, it's good to see you again." Then he stops and looks again.

"Bob Glover, Bad."

"I'll be goddamned, Bob Glover. Jesus." He takes off his glasses and pockets them. "It really is good to see you again. What the hell are you doing here, Bob?"

Bob Glover was his bass player in 1959 or 1960, one of Bad's Boys for a couple of tours during the years that Bad was on the road constantly.

"I live here. In Las Vegas. I been here nearly twenty years. I got a construction business here. I'm doing all right for myself."

"Well, hell. That's wonderful. Why the hell aren't you up here with me tonight?"

Bob Glover holds up his left hand, fingers upright and spread. "Smooth as a girl's cheek, Bad. Not a callous left. I don't play anymore. There's no time for it, the business and the kids and all. I brought someone to meet you tonight."

Bad looks down to a boy in a T-shirt, jeans and sneakers. "Howdy," Bad says. "Bad Blake's my name."

"Hello," the boy says. "Todd Glover, sir."

"Well, Todd, I'm real pleased to meet you. Did you know your dad and I used to play together?"

"Yessir."

"Grandpa, Bad. Todd here is my grandson."

"No. The hell you say."

"Sure enough." He laughs. "Tod is Bob junior's oldest."

"The hell. You had a boy. I remember that. But Bob, he wasn't any older than this boy here."

Bob laughs again. "Time has a way of slipping by. You had a boy, too."

"He's in California, with his mother. But he's . . . Hell, Bob, he's twenty-four years old now. I don't see him. I mean, since the divorce. Todd Glover"—he bends down—"how would you like to see your grandpa get up on the stage and play with me tonight? Would you like that?"

The boy nods.

"Oh no, Bad. Not this old boy. I'm a businessman now. I haven't played in years."

"Oh hell. You haven't forgotten anything. It'll come back. You bring any equipment?"

"No. Bad, I don't play."

"No problem, old buddy. We'll just kick one of these clowns out for a while. You can play guitar. You can play my guitar. I'll take the bass for a while. We can get these yahoos playing in the right tempo. Come on up. Just for a couple of songs. Hell, just for 'Slow Boat.' "

Bob laughs. "Bad, no. I can't. I won't. I appreciate the offer, but that's not my life anymore. I just came by to listen and say 'hi' and let Todd here meet you. I wanted him to see you, to know what I used to do."

"Used to do, hell. Once a musician, always a musician. You know that. It's in your blood, Bob."

"No, Bad, it's in yours. I believe that, but it's not in mine. I'm happy with my life the way it is now. I wouldn't trade it."

"Come on, Bob Glover, don't tell me you didn't have yourself a good old time when you were one of Bad's Boys."

Bob laughs. "Oh no, I'd never try to tell anyone that. I did have some real good times, but that's what they were, Bad, some good times. And it got to me. The road, you know. It wore me down. I loved it for a while, but I got tired. Remember nineteen sixty? We were on the road more than we were off. God, we'd get home and I'd see Martha and Bobby for a couple of days, start to settle in for a little bit. I mean, the dog would start to recognize me again, and then you'd call and off we'd go again. I got so I knew that bus better than my wife."

"Jesus, I loved that bus, that old Silver Eagle."

"Yeah, you did. You really did. And I really didn't. I'd have a great time the first couple of days out, then I just got tired of the road, the booze, the bars, the dope and the women. I just wanted to go home. I never understood how you did it."

"Well, hell, Bob, that's the business. When it's your business you just do it."

"Yeah, that's it. It wasn't my business. I'm a born house builder. I leave at six in the morning, and I come home at five. And twice a year I get in my Winnebago with Martha, and sometimes Todd here, and then I go on the road. Only we go fishing."

"Well, we had us some good times."

"We sure did. And I'm still proud I was one of Bad's Boys. It's a fine thing to look back on. And I'm real glad to see you're still at it. You still love it like you did?"

"I've slowed down some. I guess we all have. Mostly I stay in Houston. I've got a good little band there and steady work, but I go out every summer for a month or so. I'm the whole show now. I'm the band, the road crew and the bus driver, but yeah, I still like it."

"I hope you're easier on yourself than you were on us. You remember? Work hard, play hard? You expected everyone to work, and then, when we were done with that, you demanded everyone go play. You were like one of those slave drivers, only instead of a horse and a whip you had a guitar and a whiskey bottle."

Bad laughs and takes Bob by the shoulder. "Like I said, old buddy, I've slowed down a bit. Play one song with me and I promise I'll let you go, and get you home before sunup."

"That would be a change, but thanks just the same, I think Todd and me will just sit and listen tonight."

Bad bends back down to the boy. "Todd Glover, your grandpa here was a real good musician. I want you to know that. Him and me had some real fine times in the old days. And he could still play better than any of these guys up here with me tonight. And I'd like to buy you both a drink." He stands back up. "Coca-Cola?"

Todd nods.

"And?"

"Coca-Cola. A lot of things have changed, Bad. I don't do a lot of the things I used to do. I got a problem or two with my heart."

Bad nods. His own heart jitter-steps.

He hands them their Cokes. The band is already on the bandstand. "You sure you won't change your mind?"

Bob shakes his head and holds out his hand. "It's been great to see you again, Bad. You're still going strong. I'm real happy to see that."

"Yeah. Well, the same here. You were probably smart to get out when you did. The business has gone to the dogs. You take care of yourself. And Todd Glover, you take good care of your grandpa here. Remember, he was one of Bad's Boys. Ain't a lot of them left anymore." They shake hands.

Sweet Jesus, he thinks on the way back to the bandstand. Bob Glover a grandfather. There is another idea connected to that. He jumps up onto the bandstand and grabs his guitar. "Welcome back," he says. "Glad you stuck around. There's a lot of great music, and hell, we might never quit."

Chapter Three

He has three days in Santa Fe. He has never seen such a flat place. Buildings are built low and nestle into the hills. Even signs hug the tops of buildings. He feels he is the only vertical thing in the town.

Jack has sent two hundred dollars, waiting at the desk of the motel when he checks in. It is still morning, and he is doing errands. He has not been able to do errands in three weeks. He stops at the liquor store, and then he finds a laundry.

Back in the motel room, he unpacks, bringing most of the gear in from the van. Sitting on the bed with the television on, he brushes his white hat, working out the stains, then patting it with a cheese-cloth sack filled with chalk dust. He works on his white boots with liquid polish. The heels are getting worn, and there is a small tear near the right toe. He takes a little bottle of white glue and works it into the split with the end of a match. The boots cost him three hundred and fifty dollars two years ago. How many pairs of boots has he bought and worn out in his career?

*　　　*　　　*

He is eighteen years old. It is Louisville, Kentucky, one of the first days of spring. He has his first job, playing guitar for Eldon Morton, who has his own radio show out of Louisville and travels with his band every Friday, Saturday and Sunday to Jeffersontown and Okalona, Radcliff, Eminence, La Grange, Bardstown and Campbellville, and sometimes north into Illinois and Indiana, to Salem and Madison, Crothersville and Versailles. Bad has missed World War II, but he has a job playing for those who did not.

He is looking at his toes. They are in the first pair of pointed-toe cowboy boots he has ever worn. The boots are inside the fluoroscope machine in the middle of the shoe store. He doesn't believe those green bones are his. He is being tricked. His father warned him that people in Louisville would try to trick any boy from a place like Judah, Indiana.

He moves his toes, and inside the pointed shadows of the boots, luminous green sausages move. That makes the trick more remarkable. He moves his toes again, then, alternately, his feet. The green bones move, then the outlines of the boots. It seems that this has some connection to him. He fakes a movement with his right foot, then moves his left. In the machine, the right foot starts to move, hesitates, then the left one goes. He is trying to think of another, trickier move to confuse the machine when the salesman pulls him back and looks in the machine himself.

"They look a little tight," the salesman says. "How do they feel?"

"Fine, they feel fine."

"I guess they'll loosen with time." The salesman steps back from the machine with a smile.

Bad leans forward to look at the screen again. The green bones are pointed at the ends, but his toes are round. He has discovered proof of the trick. He realizes that people are laughing at him.

"What are you looking at in there, boy?"

"Maybe they got one of those strip-tease films running in that thing."

He looks up. Ed and Wade, who have brought him here to buy his band boots, are watching him with amusement.

"If that's it, I reckon I better have me a look," Ed says. "Eldon wants us to take care of this boy. We don't want him to get his head turned before he plays his first job." He walks over to the machine and takes a look.

34

"Nope. Ain't nothing in there but a whole mess of toes. But holy crimminy, Wade, this boy's feet are bigger on the inside than they are on the outside."

Out in the sunlight, he walks between the two men, who talk about weather and women in towns he has never heard of. He is still walking awkwardly, feeling the pull of the muscle across his shin as he walks with his toes pinched together. Walking is harder because he imagines the green bones inside his toes, glowing and scrunching as he walks. He is aware of his feet, and their movement, and in them, the bones that seem to have a separate movement of their own.

He considers calling Suzi, to tell her why her check is late. He unpacks his guitar instead and begins unstringing it. When the strings are off, he takes a bottle of polish and a cloth and rubs until he brings the luster up. Then he takes a pad of steel wool and gently works over the pickups, taking off stray spots of rust. With this done, he begins to put on new Dean Markley strings, winding each up with a plastic winder until the string nears pitch. Then he begins tightening by hand.

He brings each string up to pitch, checking it by ear. One by one, he bends the strings up, then down, to take the stiffness out, to stretch them as far as they will go. Then he retunes. When the guitar is back in tune, he moves quickly through a song he heard on the radio on the way in. It has a nice tight hook built on two note bends, and a bottom that most of the bands he gets saddled with could handle. It is a straight one, five, four, with only a couple of quick shifts to catch someone up. He doesn't remember the name of the song or the artist, but maybe he could do it as an instrumental. He can rebuild the melody.

From the outside of the bar he hears it. He stops and listens. Someone is playing piano, delicate triplet runs with the right hand over a steady rolling bass. The drummer is working behind the piano with brushes. He thinks of Smiley Robbins, who left him in—what, '63, '64? He pushes on the door and walks in, expecting to see old Smiley just sitting behind the piano, tinkering.

"Boys. Boys. He's here." The music stops and a man almost as tall as Bad walks forward. "Mr. Blake. Welcome. I'm Rocky Parker, and this is Sureshot." The big man runs through the introductions. Bad nods to each name until he gets to the last. "This here's Wesley Barnes, our piano player."

"I was listening outside." Bad shakes hands with each of the band members, coming to the piano player last. "It sounds real good. Real good." Jesus. It has been years since he has had a good piano player to work with.

Rehearsal goes slowly. Bad keeps stopping to ask if they know songs that aren't on the play list. Songs he played years before keep tumbling back to mind. Often enough the band knows them. The ones they don't, they fake pretty well. The bass is a little weak, but the drums and guitars are solid, and the piano player is a New Mexico miracle.

The band is the house band from a bar across town, which has been brought in to back him for the three nights he is in Santa Fe. Rocky Parker is an electrician. The drummer works at Montgomery Ward, and the piano player has his own tax service.

It is best to stick with the play list for tonight, Bad decides, but tomorrow afternoon they can work on some of the other stuff they have played today. Getting away from the play list will be like a vacation.

It can't be done, Rocky Parker tells him. They all have jobs. They have taken the afternoon off today, but they won't be able to do that again. After the show, Bad suggests. They can get together after the show for a few hours and work out some other numbers. That can't be done, either. The bar doesn't close until two. Rocky has to get up at six. The others work early, too. They can fake the songs they know, but they can't work out anything after this afternoon.

Bad wants to go back to the motel room and get some sleep before showtime, but he wants away from the play list, too. He is tired and hot, but he strips off his shirt and they run through five numbers three times each, until Bad figures that they are close enough for New Mexico. The band is solid, but much of the slack is being taken up by the piano player, who senses exactly what is going on and stays right with Bad. By six o'clock they have an emended play list that doesn't overjoy Bad but is the most interesting work he has done in months.

After rehearsal, he seeks out the piano player. "You're pretty good. You work before?"

Wesley Barnes is a little fat man, balding and sweating almost as much as Bad. "When I was a kid. A little. I just do this for fun. I've been playing with these guys for a couple of years now. Just weekends. Just for fun and a couple of extra dollars."

"You're good. It's real nice to run into someone on the road who really is good. It's going to be a pleasure."

"Thanks. Mr. Blake, can I ask you a favor?"

"Bad, buddy, Bad. What can I do for you?"

"You see, I have this niece. And, well, she's a writer. She's trying to be a writer. She writes for this newspaper here. I mean, it's not *The New York Times* or anything. Anyway, she'd like to do an interview with you. You know, write an article about you for the paper."

Holy Hannah, an interview. Bad has not done one for years. The ones he has done he has hated when he saw them. But damn, he has a piano player who really knows how to play.

"Well, hell yes. You send your little niece around. I'll be glad to help her out."

He is fresh from the shower, wrapped in a towel. He cracks the door to vent the shower steam and sits down to a room-service steak.

"Mr. Blake?"

He looks up. In the doorway is a woman with streaked brown hair and glasses. She is wearing a denim shirt and jeans. She looks to be in her early thirties. He is almost naked.

"I've come at a bad time."

Instinctively, he starts to stand. Then he sits again. "Who the hell are you?"

"Jean Craddock. *The Sun Scene.* Wesley Barnes's niece. I've come for an interview. This is a bad time."

"No. Yes. Shit. I'm having dinner. I just got out of the shower."

"I'll come back. When's a good time?"

"Hell. I don't know. Just wait outside for a minute. Let me get dressed."

When she leaves, he pushes the steak away and grabs for his clothes. In the bathroom he dresses quickly, trying to put his shirt and pants on at the same time. His hair is wet and combed back. He looks bald. He pushes it forward with his hand and tries to button his shirt at the same time. What the hell is he hurrying for? He is wearing his suit pants, electric blue with the lightning stripe down the leg. He has left his socks and boots in the other room. His feet look white and dead.

In the other room, there are dirty clothes and sheet music strewn all over. He pulls on one sock and hops on one foot to a pile of clothes. He bundles these up and throws them into the bathtub. He sits down

37

to pull on the other sock. He straightens the cover on the bed. There is a wet spot where he was sitting in his towel. He straightens up the sheet music, pulls on his boots and goes to the door.

"I'm sorry," she says, "I should have called. I was working another story not too far from here. I swung by on my way."

"Come in." He looks closely at her. She is older than he first thought, mid-thirties, maybe older. Her brown hair is streaked with gray and drawn into a ponytail. Behind the big glasses there are lines at the corners of her eyes. She is wearing little or no makeup, and her mouth is drawn into a tight smile that may be restrained friendliness or a smirk. She is an attractive woman. She has a tape recorder in her left hand and a camera over her shoulder. "No pictures," he tells her. "You want some steak? A potato?"

"No. How about later?"

"Which?"

"Pictures."

"Roll?"

"On stage?"

"Be all right. Mind if I eat?"

She sits across the room and sets the tape recorder on the dresser. When she crosses her legs, he sees her boots are heavy and well scuffed. His are thick with white polish. He cuts a piece of steak, puts it in his mouth and nods.

She bites her lip. "Let's see. You always dress for dinner?"

The chewed steak catches and lodges in his throat.

"Sorry. I'm sorry. Let me see. Where are you from?"

"When?"

"When?"

"Yeah, when. I'm from Houston, Texas, now. Before that I was from a bunch of other places."

"Originally."

"Judah, Indiana."

"Judy?"

"Judah. J-U-D-A-H. Folks say it Judy. I never knew why. Everyone does. I was born there. 'Bout fifty-six years ago, if that's the next question."

"Not anymore. What did you do there?"

"Grew up. Sort of. I left when I was seventeen. Before that I went to school. I hunted and fished. I ran around. I played some baseball. I played guitar and sang."

"How'd you learn music?"

"Yeah. Well, that. I don't rightly know. I just did. One day my daddy brought home an old Washburn steel-string. Someone had given it to him, or he won it off him. Or probably traded him something for it. Daddy'd trade damned near anything. Man lived to trade stuff. Stuff he'd never use in his whole damned life. That guitar. He couldn't play a lick on it. I just started fooling with it. We had a wind-up Victrola and a Philco radio, other things he had traded for. I'd just listen and try to play. Every once in a while, I'd do something right. I just sort of learned."

"You taught yourself."

"More or less. There was an old woman in church who played the piano. Miss Verna Taylor. She helped me some. Told me the names of notes, taught me what chords were, got me to read a little music, told me some theory. Later, when I was already playing, Leon Grady taught me a lot. That's when I was in Louisville. He took me to Chicago once, taught me to listen to the blues. That taught me a whole bunch."

"Who'd you listen to?"

"Oh, a bunch of people you've probably never heard of—Lulubelle and Scotty, Bradley Kincaid, Clayton McMitchum and the Georgia Wildcats. You ever hear of any of them? I didn't figure. How about Red Foley? Gene Autry, Roy Acuff? Yeah. I listened to them, too. I listened to everything."

"You learned to sing listening to them."

"Not exactly. I learned to sing in church. Everybody sang. We were Southern Baptists. I learned I could sing church songs all I wanted. If I sang radio songs around the house, my momma would hush me up. But I figured out I could walk around singing church songs all day long, loud as I could, and she'd let me be. I could sing loud enough to drown out my brother and sisters. I was the loudest damn thing in Judah, Indiana, but I was righteous loud, so it was O.K. with Momma."

He fishes the Jack Daniel's out of his pack. "Drink?"

She shakes her head.

"You don't mind if I do?"

"Of course not."

He fills a plastic glass with ice, and then fills in with the whiskey.

"Singing is all you've ever done?"

"I started when I was seventeen, and I've been at it ever since.

39

When I was a kid I had to hoe the garden and haul the washtub for the laundry, feed the chickens, that sort of thing. I figured that was enough of working. I didn't care much for it."

"What about your father?"

"He worked. I never figured he liked it much. Worked in the limestone quarry when there was work. When there wasn't, he did whatever needed doing. He worked hard. It never got him shit. You'll pardon the expression."

"I've heard it before. You never wanted to do anything else?"

"I wanted to play baseball for a while. I was pretty good at it. I thought for a while maybe I could be a musician and a baseball player at the same time. You know, sing on the radio during the winter and at night after the games were over. Then a couple of the kids learned how to throw curve balls. I decided to stick to the guitar. The damned thing stayed where it was supposed to."

"I guess it's lucky for us you never learned to hit curves."

"Lucky for me anyway. Don't get me wrong." He motions around the room. "This ain't no picnic most of the time, but I'm still doing it. A couple of years ago, my brother called me from Muncie, Indiana. He's got a car lot there. He wanted me to go in partners with him. He had it all worked out. I'd go on the television and tell all the good folks to come on down and buy one of Bad's good used cars. Hell, if I'd played baseball, I'd probably have ended up doing something like that. It's one thing to be a jerk behind a guitar, but God, to be a jerk in front of a beat-up Buick—hard to be a bigger jerk than that. You always want to be a writer?"

"Well, yes, as a matter of fact."

"You good at it?"

"Pretty good."

"You ever done anything else?"

"I was a secretary for a while. Before that I was married."

"Raising babies and all."

"Raising a husband and a construction business. I wasn't any good at it and I gave up."

"The construction business or the husband?"

"The husband. I was damned good at construction. I knew more about it than he did."

"I was never very good at being a husband. I tried it a number of times. I always gave up, too."

"You're sort of famous for that, too, aren't you?"

40

"There are some stories. They've been written before."

"I'd like to hear them from you."

"Oh hell, darlin', we don't have enough time to do my marriages."

"Five, is that right?"

"Four, actually."

"And one of your wives moved out in the middle of the night?"

"I don't know if it was the middle of the night or the middle of the day, but she moved out. That's the one you want to hear, right?"

"Yeah, I would."

"O.K. That was Marge, my second wife. It was nineteen sixty-five, in Nashville. I was drinking pretty hard in those days." He looks down at his glass. "Not like this. Hard drinking. Benders. Rolling benders. I'd start one night in Nashville and then I'd take off, through Tennessee, into Kentucky, or Missouri, down to Georgia. Once I ended up in Pennsylvania. Anyway, I'd go for about a week, sometimes longer, once or twice three weeks. And I wouldn't come home until I was flat busted. More than once I left town in a Cadillac and rode home in a Greyhound bus that I'd wired home to get the money to buy the ticket for. I'd trade a Cadillac for drinks, or just give it to someone I met.

"This went on for quite a while. She did all the usual things to get me to stop. I went to AA and to shrinks. She cried, she pleaded, she threw stuff, and she threatened to leave. And I'd straighten out for a while, but before too long I'd be drinking again, and then I'd just take off.

"Finally, I came home from one. I'd been gone a couple of weeks, I guess. I drove on home. I'd managed to hang on to the car that time, and I drove into our driveway, and it looked wrong. There was a kid's bike out there. I had a four-year-old, too young for that bike, and there was a strange dog. But none of that bothered me. I didn't think anything of it. And I walked in the front door, ready for whatever was coming, the fit, the crying, the cold shoulder. Anyway, everything was wrong. All the furniture was wrong. Nothing looked the way it was supposed to. And I just stood there, looking, trying to figure what in hell had happened. Had she got all new furniture, did I make a wrong turn and wind up in the wrong house? And the next thing I know, there is some strange woman standing in the hallway screaming. And she kept screaming.

"I got the hell out the door, and I just stood there. It was my house. Hell, I spent a fortune on it, I ought to know my own damned house.

And I started to go back in, and I thought about that screaming woman, so I just stood there on the front porch yelling for Marge. Next thing I know, the damned driveway is full of police cars and cops are crawling out of them with shotguns and pistols.

"Anyway, the point of the story is that when I took off that time, she took off, too. She called the moving company, had everything taken out of the house and put in storage, and then she rented out the house on me. And she took off. I never saw her again."

"Never?"

"Well, once. O.K.? That's the story. Now can we talk about something else?"

"I did have some questions about Tommy. Are you going to do another album together?"

"I really don't know. You want to find out, you'll have to talk to Tommy."

"Oh, come on. People want to know about Tommy Sweet."

"Look, there are a couple of things I really don't want to talk about. One is my marriages, the other is Tommy Sweet. I told you a marriage story. If you don't mind, I'd like to skip Tommy Sweet."

"O.K. Fair enough. How did you get started?"

"You sure you don't want a drink?"

"No, really. Go ahead."

"I thought reporters drank."

"Some do, some don't. Some do sometimes."

"That you?"

"Yeah. How did you get started?"

"Well, I'd lay awake at nights, listening to Momma beat on Daddy. Not hit him, but she'd get on him about his drinking and how we were poor as niggers, and why the hell didn't he do something about it besides hunt and drink. And I took a good look at him one morning. And I was just a kid but I knew he was a man who had been beat to hell, and I knew it wasn't going to happen to me. So I left home when I was seventeen. I just up and took off one night. I took some clothes, the Washburn, fourteen dollars and my baseball glove, just in case. I hitched. I got a ride as far as Louisville with a policy salesman. I was supposed to pay a dime a week. When I died, Momma would get a hundred dollars to bury me with. Anyway, the first day I was there I walked into WHM radio and told them I wanted a job singing on the radio. They laughed, of course, but there was this fellow there, Eldon Morton, who had this idea for a group and he needed another picker.

42

I thought he was some kind of hot stuff. Turns out he was hustling just like I was. But he talked himself into a radio show with a hillbilly band that sold batteries, and I was part of it. One day out of Judah, Indiana, not even twenty-four hours, and I was a Kentucky Bluebird. Three weeks after that I was on the road. I played guitar and sang a few of the harmonies. Mostly, I was big and I was young. I could fight the drunks, and there were always drunks who wanted a fight. It was the best damned training anybody could have. And I was too dumb to know it. I figured that was just the sort of thing that was supposed to happen."

"Did you make records?"

"Oh, hell no. This was strictly a radio station band. We sang on the radio in Louisville on Sunday and Tuesday nights. The rest of the week we beat through the little towns around Louisville. We sang and played, but mostly we sold auto batteries. The Kentucky Bluebirds were employed by the Bluebird auto battery company. We would do a set, and then, during the break, Eldon would tell people about Bluebird Storage Batteries, the batteries that keep you flying in blue skies. Then we'd come back and play some more. It was a wonderful time."

"And you sang?"

"Not much. I played guitar. Old Eldon wasn't any great shakes as a singer but he did most of it, what there was of it. Mostly he talked and sold batteries. Bob Wills was still around then, and Eldon had that all figured out. He had himself a bunch of pretty good musicians, and he let us do the work. I guess his major talent was finding folks who could do what he couldn't. He'd call on us to take solos. That was where the real training came in. We'd rehearse songs, solos and all. You were supposed to know you had certain solos in certain songs. But old Eldon drank quite a bit. And he'd get confused. Hell, you never knew when he was going to call on you. If he called on you by name, it was no problem. The guy who was supposed to play the solo would just play it. But if he called for the instrument—you know, guitar, piano, steel guitar—well, you played something whether you'd rehearsed it or not. My God, there you'd be, onstage or on the radio, and all of a sudden Eldon would announce you were going to play someone else's solo. You learned real fast." He takes a long pull on his drink. "I got my name from Eldon."

"Bad?"

He laughs. "Yeah. I'd only been with them for a few weeks. We were doing the radio show. He'd do that Bob Wills stuff—you know, 'Here's a man after my own heart, with a razor.' Anyway, right in the middle of 'Deep Elem Blues' old Eldon says, 'Let's hear some of that guitar from . . .' and he looks at me like he's never seen me before, and he starts over, 'some of that very good guitar from . . . ,' and it's clear he can't remember what the hell my name is, so he just says, 'from a very bad boy.' He was tighter than a pig that's got into the corncrib. Everybody in the band started calling me 'Bad Boy.' Pretty soon it was just 'Bad.' I been Bad ever since."

"What's your real name?"

"That's not for publication. I'm Bad Blake. I wasn't born Bad, and when I die I'll have my real name on my tombstone. Until then, I'm just going to stay Bad."

"That's a long time to wait for people to find out."

"Maybe, maybe not. I fight it, but age sure as hell catches up on you. It is going on the tombstone, though. I think I've got to quit being Bad when I die"—he winks—"but not until then. What time is it?"

"Eight. Ten after."

"You got enough?"

"No. I don't think so. I have more questions."

"Listen. I go on in less than two hours. I want to get ready. Maybe you can come back tomorrow and ask the rest of your questions."

"Can you give me just a half hour?"

"Really, darlin', not now. I got work to do, and I got to get ready. There are people out there who've paid good money to hear me. I always figure when all you got is the deposit slip, you better be real nice to the folks that have the checkbook."

"How about after the show?"

"Maybe; let me see. I know you got your work to do. I appreciate that. Let's see how it goes."

When she goes, he strips off his boots, shirt and pants and heads for the bed. God, he needs a nap.

Moths batter the single light bulb, strung from a wire running across the ceiling slats, held up by clinched nails. He watches the blotchy shadows skitter across the wooden floor. It is mid-June and already hot. It is early evening, still light outside, but in the house the corners where the light from the single bulb don't reach are dark. The moths have been around for a week now, large gray moths that send up clouds of dust when you hit them. They fall to the floor dead, and then minutes or hours later they are resurrected and pounding on the light bulb, trying to break their way into the single coiled white filament.

The Victrola next to him drones the song sad and slow. He picks at the strings of the big guitar. Now the song is too sad and slow, and he gets up and rewinds the Victrola, but only halfway so he can pick out the chords they are playing. He places the needle on the record and sits back down with his guitar. The Carter Family begins "Can the Circle Be Unbroken" one more time. A.P.'s voice holds the melody with a quiver, while underneath the bass notes alternate with the brushed chords. He listens to the steady alternation of the bass and brushed chords. He follows along, C, F, G⁷. When the singing stops, the bass notes walk right through the melody.

He has just come into light from a dark room. He knows, suddenly, how this thing was built, how the bass notes are picked with the thumb and the strings simply brushed with the fingers. He tries it, and he sounds right. He does it again and again, stopping to rewind the Victrola so that the song is at the tempo it is supposed to have. He works at the tempo, and when he has found it, when the alternation is regular and his fingers move to the chords without having to stop and consider what they are doing, he gets up and runs to the backyard, where his mother is picking horn worms from the tomato plants, pinching them between thumb and forefinger until the green juice spurts across her fingers. The guitar bangs against his leg as he runs. He has to play her this wonderful song about the mother who is dead.

Chapter
Four

The house is sparse and quiet. Throughout the first set, Jean
Craddock keeps edging up to the tiny bandstand to flash a
strobe light in his face. What he hears is the piano. It is like
being home. It is like being home twenty years ago. Behind him it is
like the smell of bread or the green of trees. Unexpectedly, in the
middle of "Love Like That," he steps back, nods to Wesley and lets
him go. There is no hesitation or uncertainty. The right hand weaves
the notes delicately, the sound crisp and sure. When the solo moves
to the dominant chord of the progression, Bad steps back again and
continues the break, playing the same themes, surprising himself with
sharps and flats that simply volunteer. He runs the neck in a quick
descending scale finishing with an E chord back at twelfth position and
then runs the scale again with variations. When they come back to
the chorus, the song takes off, soaring as if it were something he
hadn't heard in years.

*   *   *

At the break, a woman in a low-cut blue dress approaches, smiling. He was wonderful, she says. She heard him ten years before in Shreveport, Louisiana. He hasn't lost anything. He may, in fact, be better than he was back then. She motions to the bartender. Up near the bandstand, Jean Craddock is talking to Wesley Barnes. The woman in the blue dress hands him a Jack Daniel's, rocks. Will he play "Crazy Heart"? Of course. Her name is Ann. She works as a legal assistant, and she has loved country music all her life. She begins to recite the titles of his songs, even some B sides. Her blond hair is cut short and falls forward over her right eye. She keeps shaking her head to toss it back. If he is not doing anything after the show, they could have a late dinner, or just a cup of coffee. Jean Craddock has gone back to her table and is writing something on a long, thin pad. He thanks Ann for the drink. After the show he has promised an interview to a reporter. That's all right, Ann says, he will be in town for a couple of nights. Another time would be fine. She puts a business card in his hand and walks back to her table. Some other fans move up for handshakes and autographs. On his way back to the bandstand, Ann raises her glass as he passes.

The last set is an easy swing. They work their way through the play list methodically, no frills, no additions. With a good band behind him, the set slides by like water over stone. It is only when he is ready to move into the final "Slow Boat" that he remembers he has promised "Crazy Heart." He dedicates it to Ann, and he tries to sing it to her, though he keeps looking over at Jean. In appreciation for the drink and the damned nice thought, he plays the break slowly, bending the notes, keeping it sad and delicate. They move through that and into "Slow Boat" and out.

The size of the audience doesn't really suit an encore, so instead, he walks through the bar, between the tables, handshaking and small-talking. He gives Ann a kiss on the side of the forehead and in return gets his forearm squeezed so hard her nails dig into the flesh through his shirt.

"Are you busy now?" Jean asks. When he says no, she tilts her head and gives him a smile he can't quite read. "It looked like you were going to be busy," she says.

"No," he says. "I said I would answer some more of your questions, and I will. Help me with my stuff and we'll get started." He packs up efficiently, stopping to chat with the band, to thank and congratulate them, to say "good night, well done, and see you tomorrow." He has only the guitar and the compact amplifier. They will be safe here, the owner has assured him; they can be locked up in the backroom, and he can avoid lugging them back and forth each night. All he has left of the days when he traveled with a bus and a band and road managers to take care of the equipment is his guitar and this little amplifier. He keeps them with him. He starts to hand Jean the amplifier, changes his mind, and hands her the guitar instead.

"I can carry the amplifier, you know," she says. "I'm no fading violet. You can carry the guitar."

"It's O.K. I trust you. Just don't drop it."

As they are carrying the equipment, she says, "You said maybe."

"Maybe?"

"Maybe we'd do the interview after the show. You didn't promise."

"How many of those do you smoke in a day?" she asks as he lights another Pall Mall.

As soon as she asks, he begins to cough, a shallow cough at first, then going deeper until it begins to rattle and finally doubles him over. "Sorry," he says when he is able to catch his breath. She raises an eyebrow and then looks apologetic.

"Drink?" he asks again, fishing cubes out of the ice bucket.

This time she surprises him. "A short one. It's getting late."

"What do you want to know?" he asks as he hands her her drink.

He moves over to the bed, pulls off his boots, unbuttons his shirt and leans back against the headboard.

She looks quizzical, as if she hadn't expected the question, or didn't know what she wanted to know. "Records," she says suddenly. "What's your favorite?"

" 'Slow Boat,' " he admits. "It made me a hell of a lot of money. You can't turn your back on something that turns your whole life around like that song did. I admit I get tired of singing it twice, sometimes three times a night, but God, I'd sure hate not to have it to sing. If I didn't have it, I might not, hell, I probably wouldn't be singing anymore. I'd be in Muncie, Indiana, selling Bad's Good Used Cars for my brother. And then I'd be dead, and happy to be."

"Was it your first?"

"Oh, hell no, I had a couple dozen before that. I put 'Cheating Night Tonight' in the top ten before I did 'Slow Boat.' My first record? Let me tell you about my first record. It was a rock-and-roll song. It was back in nineteen fifty-six. Elvis had made it. And then all those other guys from Sun—Jerry Lee, Perkins, Cash. I was in Houston then, playing with another swing band, Bill Barnard's Bayou Boys. Word was out that this old boy who had a recording studio wanted to cut some rockabilly. I'd been listening to it, and I liked it. So I wrote this song, the first real song I had ever done, and I took it to him. He cut it—Bad Blake singing 'Daddy Gone.' And there I was all of a sudden, a rockabilly. I had a big pink coat with wide shoulders and lapels, and black slacks and white shoes. We never did real well with the song, sold maybe a few hundred, but I started getting out on my own, playing dances and such with my own band on the nights I wasn't with the Bayou Boys."

He runs his hand across his belly. "I didn't have all this then, but I wasn't a little Slim Jim like Elvis was, either. I went about two-ten, around there. But there I was at all these high school and college dances, swiveling my hips and toe-stepping all over the stage, swinging that guitar like it was an ax. My God, I wish you could have seen me. No, I'm glad you didn't. Thank the sweet Lord that I didn't see me."

"You liked rock-and-roll?"

"Hell yes. I liked it then and I still like it. Some of it anyway. I liked the hell out of being a rock-and-roll star. Even if I was only a rock-and-roll star in Houston."

"But you didn't stay with it."

"No. No, I didn't. Maybe I'm just country at heart. I grew up listening to country, and I started country. Even when I was doing the rock-and-roll, I was doing country, too. I mean, hell, they aren't that far apart, at least they weren't then. They get awful damned close now, too. And maybe I wasn't a real good rocker, I don't know. I know I liked it. I liked the way I did it. Maybe I didn't look rock-and-roll enough for the other folks. I never had that look. I wasn't skinny and swively like they were looking for. How many fat rock-and-rollers do you know?"

"You like country music today?"

"Not much, to be honest. There are some I like. I like some of these new kids around. John Anderson, hell, he's swiping Lefty's style, but so did Haggard, right? I like George Strait, Ricky Skaggs. They play country. Not that many do anymore. You know, the damnedest thing, Chet Atkins, who is country, real country, damned near cut the heart out of the music with his 'countrypolitan' crap. O.K.

He got a wider audience for the music. He made it what it is, but hell, he sure lost a lot of what it was, what it's supposed to be."

"And what's that?"

"Well, mostly it's supposed to be about people, what they are and what they feel. It's not just some cute saying laid over a nice, tight hook. Music today, you listen to it, say 'that's clever,' and you forget it. I get the feeling it doesn't have anything to do with anyone. At least no one I know, or would want to know."

"Who's real country?"

"Hank Williams was real country. Lefty Frizzell was real country. Roy Acuff is real country. Hank Thompson and Kitty Wells are real country. Hell, there are lots of real country people around. A lot of them are dead, but there are a whole bunch who are still around."

"Is Tommy Sweet real country?"

"More than he'll admit to. When he started, he was as country as you could get. He was so damned country, traffic lights confused him. He started playing country with me. I taught him country. He tries to cover it up a lot, but yes, Tommy is country. When I was growing up, I ate a lot of rabbit. Sometimes it was the only meat we got for weeks, for months—rabbit, possum, squirrel. When I left home, I swore I would never eat another rabbit or squirrel as long as I lived. Now I eat steak. I dream about rabbit, but I won't eat it. No matter how it's fixed. That's sort of the way Tommy is about country music. Maybe someday he'll come around. He did it with me on *Memories*. I'll tell you this, enough of these kids doing country make some money, Tommy'll be back in overalls and bare feet before long."

"How did you meet Tommy?"

"Look, darlin', I don't want to be cantankerous, but like I said, I really don't want to talk about Tommy, O.K?"

"O.K. What do you want to talk about?"

"Where are you from?"

"Originally?"

"Yeah, where are you from?"

"Enid, Oklahoma. Why?"

"That's what I want to talk about."

"Enid, Oklahoma?"

"No. You. I been to Enid, by the way."

"Depressing, isn't it?"

"I'm playing in Benson, Arizona, in a couple of nights. Nothing depresses me anymore. Why'd you leave?"

"It depressed me. And I was young and in love."

"You can be in love anywhere. I've done it in all kinds of places."

"I guess so, but when the one you're in love with is hell-bent to get out of Enid, Oklahoma, and you're not real crazy about it, either, it doesn't take much to get you out."

"That your husband?"

"Yeah. He was going to build the West."

"Did he?"

"Some of it. A lot of houses here. A couple of shopping centers."

"Why'd you leave him?"

"Hold on just a minute. I'm supposed to be the one asking the questions here, and if I can't ask you personal questions, you sure as hell can't ask me any."

"If I let you ask me some, can I ask you some?"

"Why?"

"You're nice. I don't get to talk to that many nice people. Another drink?"

"One more. Short and quick. You haven't told me the story about how dear old what's-his-name stepped aside one night and let you be the front man for a while."

"What the hell story is that?" He hands her her drink.

"The story I get from everybody I've ever interviewed in this business. They always start as a sideman, then the star gives them their big break and they become stars."

"And I forgot to tell you that one? My lord, the Brotherhood of Nashville Nose and Guitar Pickers will have my behind for missing that one."

"You mean it never happened?"

"Not exactly. When I was cutting those rockabilly records in Houston, we were sending them out around the country. I cut a couple of straight country numbers, too, and Wilson Cruthers from Federation heard one and offered to let me cut a demo for Federation. They liked it and signed me. The third one I cut for them was 'Cheatin' Night Tonight.' Things kind of went from there. I was a sideman and all, but not for anyone famous, and those I played with wouldn't have stepped aside when the Red Sea parted."

"What ever happened to Federation?"

"J.M.I. bought them out in nineteen sixty-two. I recorded for them for another five years, then they cut me loose."

"And now?"

He looks around the room. "And now, this. I've cut a couple for a little independent in Houston, but mostly I've given up on that. The independents can't compete with the conglomerates. It's a whole bunch of people who bust their asses to put out a quality product that can't get airplay. That's controlled by a bunch of yahoos with gold jewelry and Mercedes cars who only care about Jacuzzis and each other's secretaries and how much money they can stick up their noses. Music is just a diversion for them. Hell, I ain't going to sweat for them. Except for the duet with Tommy, I don't really record anymore. What else?"

"What time is it?"

"I don't know, still early."

"It wasn't early when we started this. It must be three or four by now."

Bad digs his watch from the drawer beside the bed. "No, it ain't that late."

"How late?"

"It ain't four yet. It's hardly three."

"It's late enough. I better go."

"I thought reporters stayed with a story until they got it."

"I've got an awful lot now."

"There's a lot more. Hell, I'll tell you stories that will make your readers laugh, cry, shiver, scream and lock up their daughters. I'd keep digging until I cave in and confess, if I was you."

"Really, I better go. You've been awfully nice. I've enjoyed this."

"Me, too. Honestly."

"You know, it's odd finally meeting you and talking with you."

"Odd?"

"Odd. I've heard you for years. Wesley is a real fan of yours. I listened to him talk about you and play your songs. I sort of felt like I knew you."

"Now you do. And I know you, and that's my pleasure."

"Well, thanks. You've been kind. Maybe I'll see you again before you leave?"

"Can I ask you one more of those personal questions?"

"I guess."

"Will you stay? Here? With me?"

"I'm sorry. No. I can't. You're very nice, but no. Really. Thank you."

"I'd like you to."

55

"I know. I mean, I believe that. But I just can't."

"Boyfriend?"

"No. Boy, four. He's with a baby-sitter. I've got to go rescue both of them. You turned that woman in the bar down. I'm sorry. I really am. I didn't mean to spoil anything."

"Don't be, it's O.K. I get offers in bars most nights. I don't get nice reporters from Enid, Oklahoma. This was better. I mean that. You go on home to your boy. It's O.K."

He pours himself a drink while she packs up her recorder and notes. "I hope that comes out well." He nods to the recorder.

"I put in new batteries."

"See, not only nice and pretty, but smart, too. Make sure I get a copy when you get it done. Here, let me give you my address." She hands him a pad and her pencil. He writes his Houston address. Then he hands it back to her. When he leans, she leans. When he kisses her she moves in tight. He runs his hand along the twin ridges by her spine. She holds the kiss, then breaks.

"Oops. Sorry, cowboy. I guess I got carried away. I have a baby-sitter to rescue."

When she is gone, he begins to straighten up. He takes his coat from the back of the chair and puts it in the closet. He reaches into the side pocket and pulls out the business card. Ann Ralston, Legal Assistant. Above her work number, she has inked in another number. He looks at the card and then at his watch. It is a quarter to four. He puts the card back in his pocket. Oddly, he doesn't feel any regret.

It is mid-June, sticky hot in the white clapboard church. He has come in late, squeezed onto the wooden pew next to his sister. Around him he hears the drone of flies, lazy in the heat, describing wide sloping arcs above their heads. Around him, pasteboard fans on thin sticks are snapped by the fat wrists of sweating women, breaking small breezes against thick night air.

"The Old Rugged Cross" is winding down, the last notes descending into the lower register, rumbling in the throats of men whose faces, red from neck to forehead, white from forehead to hairline, are glistening with sweat. He gets in the last note, and with the rest, sits down.

While the others look to the front of the church where Brother Randall is slowly easing his bulk up to the podium, he looks down, checking his fingers for yellow tobacco stains. He keeps his head down, avoiding breathing in his sister's direction, where she might smell the corn whiskey.

"The time has come," Brother Randall says, "for us to make a choice. This is the time. Not tomorrow or the day after or the week after or the year after." He drops his voice to barely a whisper, but a whisper that rushes out and covers the whole church. "This is the time. And it is a simple choice. You don't have to mull it over. You don't have to think on it, sleep on it, or discuss it with your neighbor or the banker. The choice is clear. It is the choice, brothers and sisters, of spending all eternity wrapped in the arms of those you love, those who love you, especially in the arms of Jesus Christ our Lord, whose love is greater than anything you and I can even begin to imagine. A choice to move into the light of that promise, the greatest promise ever made, the promise that will be kept now and for all time."

Around him, the air has grown denser and wetter. It sinks into his lungs and he has to push it out. When he has pushed it out, more wells over him and sinks into him and he pushes. Sweat gathers and drips in his ears and from the tip of his nose, and the smell of his sweat gathers and combines with the smell of other sweat and the smell of his sister's lilac toilet water. It stings his eyes and clogs his nose. And beneath it all, the other smell that comes welling up from him. He is getting sick with it; he folds his arms across his stomach and bends forward.

"Such a simple choice. To rest yourself forever and all time in the greatest love, or to fall naked into the everlasting flames that burn and blacken but never consume. The flames that keep biting and burning. And there is no way out. There is no water that will drown the flame, no blanket to smother it.

"When I was just a boy I watched a barn burn. And in that barn, there was a horse trapped. And there was no way to get through that fire to save that poor animal. And I still think of the horse, caught in the burning barn, screaming and terrified. And I think of the sound and the smell, the terror and the pain of that horse. But then I think, those flames, brothers and sisters, consume. And after the minutes of that animal's terror and suffering, he was released, and it was over, and it will never return. And then I think once more. I think of the flames that do not consume, that burn and burn, and the smell and the terror and the agony that is never over. The burning from which there is no release."

The whiskey is moving now. It begins to churn in his stomach and crawl up his throat. And from his crotch the smell of sex keeps rising, overpowering the sweat and the lilac toilet water and coming up in great waves that roll over him. He crouches over harder, trying to keep the smell and the whiskey contained in himself.

"But there is release, and the release is now. Make the choice, brothers and sisters. Open your hearts and receive Him here, tonight, this minute, and you will have your release. He asks so little of you. Open your heart to Him, and He will open His heart to you. The heavenly release is yours for so little. Step forward and take Him for your savior and have your release. Know that your trials, your pain, your suffering, will find release and you will be free. Step forward now. Accept Him. Let Him accept you. Step forward now."

His sister's elbow catches him in the arm and straightens him up. As she rises, he rises, and she pushes him out of the pew and into the aisle, where the people are beginning to move forward. Around him, they move, their eyes locked forward, up toward Brother Randall, up toward the salvation and release, and the smell and the whiskey push upward at him and spin him around until he is facing the people moving forward, all people he knows, who do not show any sign of recognition but keep their heads forward, eyes locked toward the front. He begins pushing his way through, easing past a woman in a cotton dress with small light-blue figures, and then square into a man in white cotton shirt and Cant-Bust-Em overalls. He pushes past and runs into more, as the congregation starts moving forward. He pushes and pushes until he is running, down the aisle and out the door and onto the dirt in front of the church.

The air is suddenly chillingly cool on his sweating skin, and he runs a few more yards toward the maple tree before he lurches forward onto his knees and begins to puke whiskey. It keeps coming, more than he could possibly have drunk, burning his nose and throat. Finally, he is convulsed. The waves coming up from his stomach bring nothing with them. He pushes away, then falls again and rolls onto his back, looking up at the stars that burn forever.

And then his mother is standing over him, her jaws clenched in fury. "How dare you," she says, "how dare you come into the House of the Lord like that. You get out of here, get. You are no better than him. You are no better than your father. You don't care about anything but liquor and women. And you are growing up just like him. Neither of you are any better than a damn nigger. You're going to spend your life nigger poor, just like he done."

When the phone rings, Bad does not know where he is. "Mr. Blake," the familiar voice says, "hold for Mr. Greene." Bad rolls over for his watch, then a Pall Mall. It is eleven o'clock.

"Bad," Jack says, "how are you?"

"It's eleven o'clock in the morning, Jack. I'm dead."

"How's Santa Fe? It's a great town. You been to the Palace of the Governors yet?"

"Jack, it's eleven o'clock in the fucking morning. I haven't even been to sleep yet."

"Wake up, Bad. I've got great news. You're going to like this. Get out of bed and get a pencil and paper."

"Shit." Bad rolls out of bed and stumbles to the dresser. In a drawer, he finds a postcard of the motel. He looks for a pencil, but he can't find one. He can't find his glasses, either. He goes back to the phone. "Hold on, I can't find a goddamned pencil." There are pencils out in the van, but it is downstairs and a couple of hundred yards away.

He lights another match and lets it burn. Then he blows it out, and goes back to the phone. "O.K., what do you have?"

"Cancel Benson, Arizona, on your itinerary."

He still hasn't found his glasses, so he scrawls in big letters on the back of the postcard, "CAN BEN," with the burnt match. "What the hell is so great about canceling another stop?"

"Wait till you hear what I've got for you instead. Are you ready for this? Are you writing this down?"

Bad looks at the burnt match. He figures it's good for a few more letters. "Yeah, I'm writing this down. What am I writing?"

"You won't believe this. I busted my ass for this. Write it down—the twenty-ninth, Phoenix, Arizona, Veterans Memorial Coliseum, eight-thirty."

Bad writes "PHO, VET MEM," before the match gives out.

"Well?" Jack says.

"Well what?"

"Bad, for Christ's sake. I just called to tell you you're out of the Horseshoe Lounge in Benson, Arizona, on the twenty-ninth, and instead you're in a goddamned arena in Phoenix. For Christ's sake, Bad."

"An arena?"

"A goddamned arena, Bad. Ten thousand seats. I got you opening a major show in Phoenix."

"Opening? Shit. I don't open."

"Cut the crap. This is ten thousand seats we are talking about, and in slack times. Where the hell else are you going to play ten thousand seats? Bad, this is the biggest damned thing you've done in years. Don't tell me you don't open. There are acts up the bedudah that would kill to open for ten thousand seats."

"Opening for who?"

"This is the best part. Tommy Sweet."

"Shit." He can't think of anything else to say. "Shit," then, "Fuck," then, "No. No goddamned way."

"Bad. Look. Think about this. You want to do another album with Tommy. This is a step in the right direction. Open for him, get together, talk with him. I haven't been able to convince him, but I got him to agree to this. It's a first step, damn it. You can convince him. Let him hear you. Hell, you can pull it off. It's ten thousand seats, Bad."

"Goddamn it, Jack, I won't do it. I'll open for someone else. Find someone else and I'll open, but not Tommy."

"Who else are you going to open for? Who's playing arenas these days? Willie Nelson, Kenny Rogers and Tommy Sweet—that's who. Who the hell are you going to open for? Springsteen? You want to open for Springsteen? How about Madonna? Should I try Madonna? This is it, Bad. This is the break we've been waiting for. Don't get stubborn and blow the whole damned deal."

"Oh, goddamn, Jack. I don't know. Tommy. Hell, I can't open for Tommy."

"This is a grand and a quarter for one night. This is ten thousand seats. A quarter of those never heard of you, another quarter figure you're dead. That's five thousand people you can bring around, and another five thousand that haven't been thinking a lot about you the last few years. This is exposure, Bad. This is the best exposure you're going to get."

"I just don't know, Jack."

"Look, Bad. I'm talking business here. That's what you pay me for. I went out and busted my ass for this, and damn it, I got it. You got it. We beat a couple dozen acts on this one. You better start thinking business here and forget pride for a while. Besides that, Tommy wants you. He really does."

"Jack, the dream of every sideman in the whole fucking world is that someday the front man whose ass he's been staring at for months, for years, is going to open for him. I don't owe that dream to Tommy Sweet. I don't owe Tommy Sweet one fucking thing."

"That's right, Bad. You don't owe Tommy Sweet a damned thing. You and I both know that Tommy owes you. Well, he's making a payment here, Bad. He's offering you the chance to open for ten thousand seats. He's offering you the biggest audience you're going to get right now. He's offering you a grand and a quarter. Maybe he's thinking of offering you another album. Don't be so damned stubborn. Let him pay off a little bit. You've tried to take your damned pride to the bank before, Bad, and you and I both know exactly how much it's worth."

"Goddamn. Goddamn you, you motherfucking, cocksucking son-of-a-bitch."

"You'll do it?"

"I don't know. Goddamn it, Jack, if you were here right now, your lips would be on the back of your head. Let me think about it. I'll call you back."

"No. Tell me now."

"I need time to think. I'll call you this afternoon."

"There is no time. Tell me now."

"Jack, let me think. Goddamn, please let me think."

"Yes or no, Bad."

"Goddamn . . ."

"Yes or no?"

"Yes. Goddamn it, yes."

"Good. Now listen. I'll get you a good backup band. I promise. You'll have the best available. You'll be billed in all the ads that run from now on. Be at the coliseum by twelve noon for rehearsal and sound check. Check with Ralphie. He's Tommy's road manager. He'll have everything set up for you. You getting all this?"

Bad looks at the stub of burned match. "Yeah, right. I'm getting all this. Have Brenda send me an itinerary."

"Don't mess this up."

"Jack," he says, tired now, "I told you. I'll do it. Have I ever backed down on a promise to you?"

61

"No, Bad. No, you haven't. And you'll do a good show. And it's going to come off well. I know you. Have a good time, Bad."

"Right. It's like I get great seats for a Tommy Sweet show, right? And I get to go backstage and meet him in person and everything?"

"You'll be great. I know you will."

"You bet your sweet ass."

"So how are things in Santa Fe, anyway?"

"I've got a piano player. He's good. He's fucking good."

"A piano player? That's nice, Bad. That's real nice. Listen, I have another call on the line. I'll be talking to you."

"Right." When the line is dead, he hangs up the phone. Tommy Sweet, Jesus Lord, you got me opening for Tommy Sweet.

He has opened before. He has opened for Ray Price, Jim Reeves and Roy Acuff. When he was still in Louisville, the Kentucky Bluebirds opened for Hank Williams. He shook Hank Williams' hand, he took a drink of bourbon from Hank Williams' bottle. Hank Williams, a skeleton in a Nudie suit, said to him, "You can pick some guitar there, Slim." Now he will open for Tommy Sweet, who used to back him.

Chapter
Five

Chapter
Five

After he picks up his laundry, folded and wrapped in brown paper, his suits, red, yellow and orange, under clear plastic, he drives into the middle of town. The streets are narrow and lined with cars. The Palace of Governors is a long, flat building built from mud and braced by cedar posts. Along the sidewalk, under the portico, Indians display their jewelry, baskets and trinkets on blankets. There must be some joke here, Bad thinks. How the white men got so much away from the Indians by giving them beads and trinkets, and here they are trying to get some of it back by selling the white folks from Iowa and Connecticut and Pennsylvania beads and trinkets. When he looks closely at the faces of the old Indian women, he decides there is no joke here of any kind.

Down from the palace is the cathedral, hundreds of years old, built by Spanish monks. He walks around the garden, marveling at what these people were able to accomplish with mud and cedar. On impulse, he opens a side door and walks in. Inside, the cathedral is huge and empty, except for pews and altar. It is painted in earth tones, tan, pink and turquoise. Rows of columns support a vaulted ceiling of pink squares edged with thin lines of turquoise. At the front is the altar, behind a cedar railing. On one side, a large white marble Virgin; on the other, a crucifix with a twisted, tortured Christ. His Baptist upbringing has never prepared him for this graphic representation of Christ in agony. Around him, the columns begin to soften and slowly bow. The vaulted ceiling trembles and begins slowly to lower. The outer walls follow the ceiling, leaning in at the top, down toward him, until the whole church is beginning to lower around him, to enfold and smother him. His heart begins its awkward race, missing beats here and there, and his breath comes in hard, wheezing gasps. He is cold, and his shirt is wet with sweat. Around him, the bright room darkens. He is suddenly outside, in bright sunlight, unsure what has happened, struggling to control his breathing. The wall of the cathedral behind him is cool and solid against his wet back. He lurches away from it, and into the garden.

East of Santa Fe, he revives. He is less than twenty miles out of town, on a plateau of the Sangre de Cristo Mountains, overlooking the Mora River sliding slowly past, fifty feet below him. Also below him, cars wind past on the snaking blacktop. From the top of the plateau, he hears only wind pushing through the leaves of scrub oak. His boots crunch softly through dirt and dry brush as he walks past. Ahead of him, a jay scuttles from bush to bush, quietly watching him, tilting its head from side to side.

He has his heartbeat under control, his breathing is regular. The sweat has cooled and dried on his face and neck. He squats and plucks blades of dry grass, braiding them together. Once in 1967 in Nashville, he went to the wedding of one of Lee Stoner's sidemen. Before the ceremony, he felt the eyes of Jesus, twisted on the cross, unlock from their upward imploring and take hold of his own, augering into him, until he had to brace himself on the pew in front of him, locking his elbows and gritting his teeth, straining not to be pulled straight forward and up toward the bleeding Jesus for some accounting he was not, would never be, prepared to give. Then the cross and body started to torque, twisting loose from the marble base to come at him and for him. Christ twisted at the horizontal arms of the cross, trying to wrench it free, to free himself to get at Bad, and Bad pushed his way down the pew and into the aisle, running past ushers and guests to get to the fresh air and sunshine, where he fell on his knees, breath coming in long gulps.

Until today, he has not been in a church since. The churches of his boyhood, the plain and simple white wooden shells filled with wooden chairs, where the sermons of damnation were smoothed over and softened by the singing of dozens of voices in praise and thanksgiving, have given over to the tall, angular structures of blame and redemption. Bouquets of wildflowers have been replaced by statues of Jesus, racked and bleeding, looking upward as if asking who has done this to Him. As soon as he walks into one of these churches, Bad can feel Jesus' eyes break loose in their plaster sockets and swivel toward him, claiming, I know. What a friend we have in Jesus.

The wind picks up. To the south, over the tree-topped hills, gray clouds are starting to build. The wind has an edge to it. If he doesn't look down toward the river and road, but off toward any horizon, he can see only trees and sky. Voices rise around him and he is lifted into the rhythm of singing: "With my Jesus on high, / Where we never shall die, / In the land where we'll never grow old."

The Friday night house is nearly full. Sureshot has been playing for over an hour when Bad, wearing black slacks, white shirt and black hat, climbs up onto the stage. While the band is working through a verse of "Last Cheater's Waltz," Bad crouches behind the amplifiers, plugs in and checks his tuning. As Rocky Parker begins the chorus, Bad walks up behind him and sings a bass harmony. From the bar, there is scattered applause. He tips his hat. At the end of the chorus, he simply joins the band for the rhythm. It has been months since he has enjoyed playing enough to just walk up and join the band before his own set begins. He plays two more numbers with them, trading licks with Wesley Barnes on "Funny, How Time Slips Away," and then leaves the stage to the band until they are ready for his set.

He sits at the bar and while the band plays "Every Time Two Fools Collide," he sips his drink, nodding and smiling to customers who catch his eye. No one comes up to shake hands or talk. As the band breaks into the final number of the set, "Rocky Top," he impetuously slides off his barstool, takes the hand of a woman at the table next to him and leads her onto the dance floor. They do a quick, nearly graceful shuffle with lots of spins as the tempo of the song increases incrementally. By the time the song is over, he is huffing and wheezing, dizzy, his face burning from the exertion. Around the bar, people stand and clap. Bad and his partner bow to each other and the audience. He is actually having fun.

During the break, he gets surrounded, handshaken, patted and pounded. Across the room he catches a glimpse of Jean, but people crowd toward him, blocking his view. Behind him on the bar, half a dozen drinks are lined up for him. He takes a couple of sips from each before it is time to hit the stage.

"Thank you, Santa Fe," he says from behind the light. "My God, what a beautiful place you've got here." He moves into "A Cheatin' Night Tonight," and the first set moves by quickly. A woman in jeans and T-shirt brings a beer to the bandstand for him. "Darlin'," he says, "that's just real sweet, but I just can't drink that beer." He turns sideways, so they can see his profile. "I got to protect this fine figure I worked so hard for."

Drinks keep appearing through the break. Bad keeps chatting with people who come up to meet him, and he manages to get only a couple of mouthfuls down. He keeps looking for Jean, but he can't find her. When the stage lights are on, his vision is obscured by glare and dark; when the house lights are on, people are up and milling around.

"What do you all think of Sureshot?" he asks to open the second set. When the audience breaks into applause, he says, "Aren't they a fine bunch? I think so much of them, I think we ought to kick out the play list this set and play a little Stump the Band, don't you?" More applause. "What would you like to hear?"

"Slow Boat" comes up several times, a couple of other standards, before Bad hears the oddball he has been waiting for. "Sir?" he asks. "Did you really call for 'White Lightnin' '? Do you know that's George Jones's song? Do you know I'm not George Jones?" The guy keeps grinning and clapping. "Do you know which side of you your chair is on?" The guy grins and claps. "Well," Bad says, "I guess he's passed the sobriety test, and I guess we better do 'White Lightnin'.' " The drummer gives him the tempo. "Hold it, hold it," he says. "We didn't rehearse this, but if we're going to wing it, let's really wing it." He counts the beat back to the drummer, sped up by half.

In the song, he forgets the last verse, but in the chorus he pulls the "White Lightnin' " refrain up basso profundo, and in the break, he and Wesley just start to cut. He plays runs he hasn't played in years, and Wesley keeps pushing him, finding new phrasings of the melody that demand answers. All in all, they stretch the song to over five minutes.

After "White Lightnin'," the crowd begins asking for odder, and faster, stuff—Elvis, Hank Cochran, Jerry Lee Lewis, Hank Thompson. By the time they get to Bare's "Marie Laveau," he has the audience whooping into the chorus with him. After the song, Rocky Parker surprises him, telling him they have only ten more minutes to get offstage before last call. They bring it down on "Slow Boat."

"Wait," he says. "One more, let's do one more." Then to the band, " 'Satisfied'?" Wesley Barnes nods and leads it off. "I got that old-time religion," Bad sings, "that old-time religion, / And that is why I'm satisfied." Wesley Barnes has moved into boogie, and the audience, bewildered at first to hear gospel in a bar, has begun to clap along with the band. "I'm satisfied, / No trouble will ever get me down. / When my eyes are closed in death, / With my Jesus, I'll be at rest, / And that is why I'm satisfied." He follows with a double descending run, going suddenly and surprisingly sharp on the last note, and he is out. "Thank you, good night, and God love you all."

He is packing up, winding the guitar cord, hand to elbow, stowing it in the back of the amplifier, when she moves forward. "That was wonderful," she says. She is at the edge of the bandstand in a straight white dress cinched at the waist by a concho belt. She looks different, more handsome than he remembers.

"Hey," he says, "more questions?"

"A couple, if you don't mind."

He picks up the guitar and amplifier. "Which one do you want?"

"Since I have a choice, let me stick with the guitar."

"Drink?" he asks again when they get to his room.

"Sure." She unpacks her recorder and sets it on the dresser.

"That's a real nice dress."

She smiles, starts to respond, then begins again. "Why did you do that?"

He stops pouring the bourbon. "Do what?"

"Sing that gospel song. I mean, a gospel song in a bar."

"Did you like it?"

"Of course. It was wonderful. But I've never heard anybody do anything like that. It was terrific. I mean, how did you know you could get away with something like that?"

He lights a cigarette. "I knew. I knew I could get away with anything tonight. I just decided to do it. Sometimes it works. Maybe it's you, or maybe the audience, or the stars or vibrations or whatever the hell you think it is. Sometimes it just works. Tonight it worked.

'Satisfied' is a great song. It's not a great gospel song, it's a great song, period. It feels real good. I felt good, so I did it."

"Are you religious?"

"I was. Maybe I still am, I don't know. I don't go into churches if I can help it. I don't say my prayers at night anymore. But I guess I believe there's a God, and I guess I believe He keeps track. If that's religious, I'm that. You religious?"

She shakes her head.

"But you liked the song. See, it doesn't make any difference, it's a great song. It's sort of the way with country music. There really isn't any forbidden territory. You can sing about anything. I mean, we got all these drinkin' and fightin' and lovin' and cheatin' songs. As long as it's something that people feel, it's O.K. for country music. So it's O.K. to sing gospel in a bar. I felt happy, and it's a happy song that makes other people happy, so I wanted to play it. I don't say this stuff very well. Maybe you can fix it up so it makes sense in your paper."

"I think you did O.K."

"You know I don't know much about books and stuff. I know movies, mostly. But books and movies, they make life glamorous, you know? Lives come out better, or bigger, than they are. But in books they write about special kinds of people. Country music is about people who aren't real special, who are never going to be. They grow up, work, get married, slip around, and they die. And the music is the glamour of that kind of life. Maybe slipping around on your wife or husband ain't the best thing in the world, but for a lot of folks, it's what they got. And the music, it helps."

"What about your songs?"

"I try."

"I mean, where do you get them?"

"Out of living. Where else? What else can you write about?"

"Like 'Slow Boat.' Where did that come from?"

"Marge. My second wife. The one that run off. That's her song."

"Did you write songs about all your wives?"

"All my wives and a bunch of others."

"Like which?"

"Songs or others?"

"Songs."

"Well, let's see. 'Love Came and Got Me,' that was with Evelyn, my first wife, then 'It's Strange' was Kathryn, number three, and 'Love Like That' was for Suzi, my last wife."

70

"Number four."

"Number four, the last. It's the same thing."

"It's funny. You know, those are all happy songs, real love songs. Yet you've broken up with four different wives. Didn't you write any of the sad ones?"

"Hell yes, only you've never heard them. I only recorded a couple of them. I don't write those songs very well. I do a lot of them—'Faded Love,' 'Please Release Me,' 'Crazy Heart,' things like that. But the ones I wrote just don't work. Hank Williams wrote better about endings than beginnings. With me it's just the opposite. Hank's songs are really pretty. Mine are like endings—ugly."

"What do you mean?"

"Well, maybe this has happened to you. I hope it hasn't. But there are times you are in bed, you know, I mean making love, and something's wrong, and then you realize that for the other person, this is just practice. I mean, I can't make a song out of that."

"That means you've tried?"

"Yes. Yes, that was Suzi. She was twenty-three and I was forty-six, forty-seven, and she started out thinking I was something pretty wonderful—a genuine country-western star. It didn't take her a whole lot of time to figure out what she had was a broke-down singer and picker who wasn't ever going to take her to Hollywood or New York City."

"I don't know. You don't seem that broke down."

He looks at her, really looks at her. Besides trading in the jeans and denim shirt for the dress, she is wearing her hair down, and a trace of makeup. She looks younger than last night, softer, and she smiles, not more but more fully. "Is this what you really want to talk about?"

"No. I guess not."

"You got a baby-sitter tonight?"

She nods her head. "He's with a friend."

"You stay?"

"If you still want me to."

He moves toward her, and she meets him halfway. As he starts to put his arms around her, he realizes he has a drink in one hand, a burning cigarette in the other. Somehow, in all the years, this has never stopped being awkward. By the time they break their kiss, he has dumped ashes in his drink, and she has dribbled hers down the back of his leg.

71

"That pretty white dress," he says, "would still look pretty on that chair there."

After the urgency of snaps and buckles, hooks and zippers, comes the urgency of unfamiliar skin and contours. When she is naked, he can't let go of her and holds her close while she tries to get his clothes off. She unsnaps his shirt and works it over his arms, works his belt buckle open, then tugs down his pants and shorts, only to realize he is still wearing his boots.

"Let me," he says. His pants are around his ankles, and he can't bend down to the boots without losing his balance and falling.

"Here," she says, and pushes him back until he is sitting on the bed. Then she begins to wrestle off the boots. He does his best to help her, trying to straighten his foot so the boot will slide off. But that only raises his instep, wedging it tighter in the boot.

She had begun gracefully, bending over to tug at the boot. He had watched the soft sway of her breasts. Now she is doubled over, not tugging, but pulling at the boot, turning and working her arms around it, like a pipefitter working on a froze-up valve. She swings one leg over his and pushes at the boot, then swings the other over and keeps pulling until it slides off, and she ends up on the floor, sitting facing him, legs spread, arms full of cowboy boot, hair in her face, and a smile of triumph.

In spite of himself, he is laughing. On the floor, she doesn't look naked or sexy, but like a child who has just completed a simple chore.

"I think I better do the other," he says.

"You're damned right," she says, then, noticing his withering erection, "Oh hell."

"You come here. Everything will be all right, as soon as I get this damned boot off."

After the initial rush of passion, they slow and luxuriate, then grow shy. He gets up for drinks and a cigarette and puts on his shirt to walk the eight feet to the dresser. She pulls up the sheet and tucks it around her.

"That was nice," she says.

"That was something more than nice." She leans into his arm, and he touches her hair with his fingers. "You're very beautiful."

"No," she says. "But thank you. I'm a lot of things, but I was never beautiful."

"You are," he insists. "And I would bet you've gotten more so over the years."

"Is this the famous country charm I've heard so much about?"

"I guess I wouldn't know a whole lot about that. I've never been real famous for charm. Country or any other."

"But you're famous. What's that like?"

"What's being a reporter like? Sometimes it's nice. A lot of times it's a pain in the butt. When people know who you are, they think they know who to ask for whatever they think they want. I never figured out whether I liked it or not. I started out wanting to be rich and famous. Then I was. Then I wasn't. I guess I want to be again. I don't know. I'd like to have another hit. I'd like people to know I can still do it."

She raises her glass. "I'll testify to that."

"Reporter's charm?"

"Reporters aren't famous for charm, either." She tilts her head up to kiss him.

He eases the sheet down from her breasts. She grips it and then relaxes. "I guess I don't have anything to hide anymore, do I?"

"That's maybe the best part, not hiding for a while." He continues working the sheet down, following it with his lips and tongue, over breasts and ribs, belly, over the lateral scar. "You really are beautiful," he says.

"Don't talk."

He wakes from dreamless sleep. Her head is cradled on his arm, her breathing regular and shallow on his chest. Love starts this way always, waking, his arm pleasantly numb from being slept on all night. And it always ends trying, in sleep, to get as far away as possible, until no bed is big enough to get the necessary distance. It always starts in sleep before it works its way into waking and consciousness.

It is still early, he knows, the room full of deep shadows. He gently lifts her head and eases his arm out from underneath. She stirs and groans, but her breathing eases and flattens out. He gets up and puts on his pants. He calls room service for coffee to be left outside the door. He lights a cigarette, moves their clothes from the chair and sits, watching her sleep.

"You could call in sick," he says.

"Don't think I wouldn't like to. I don't exactly have seniority on the paper. If I let up, I'm going to end up out on my ass. Besides, when you stick around, you get the good stories. I'm tired of movie reviews

73

and interviews with the county agricultural agent on thrip control."

"And fading country singers."

She is sitting on the bed, in her slip, eating toast. She stops to lick a drop of butter from the side of her hand. "I worked to get this interview. It was my idea—well, Wes's actually, but I pitched it and got it. I thought it would be fun." She smooths strawberry jam over the toast. "My God. I had no idea how much fun it was going to be."

"Best damned interview I ever got."

"No one can say Jean Craddock doesn't throw herself into her work, or at least at her work."

"I got something else you can use if you still need something."

"I haven't put it together yet. What is it? Something salacious, I hope."

"Actually, no. I'm opening for Tommy Sweet in Phoenix in a couple of days."

"That's great." She looks puzzled at his expression. "That's not great, is it?"

"It's great," he says. "My agent has told me how great it is. It's good money, it's exposure. But hell, it's a hard thing, you know, opening for the guy who used to be your sideman. Hell, I gave that kid his start."

"What is it between you two?"

"It's that. I taught him how to sing and I taught him how to play. I got his teeth fixed. I got him exposure, I even helped him go out on his own. Son-of-a-bitch won't return my phone calls. Next time you see him grinning at you from one of those album covers, think about this: those teeth are mine. I bought and paid for them. Soon as things started to pop for him, he never looked back. Not a thank you, not even a damned Christmas card."

"But you did an album together."

"We did a hell of an album together. My agent did that. Tommy was cutting duet albums right and left. Jack just convinced him that that was the logical thing to do. He got sixty-five percent of the son-of-a-bitch, too. I put that album together. He cashed most of the checks."

"He is good, though."

"He can be good. He used to be good. He doesn't work at it hard enough. When he started out, he was the hardest damned worker I ever saw. I really liked that. But now he just sort of slides by. You noticed how flat he is on the new albums?"

"No. I guess I haven't really noticed."

74

"Most people don't. They hear the voice, recognize the phrasing, that's Tommy Sweet and they're satisfied. Yeah, he's always sung flat. In the old days, he used to work past it. He used to work and work until he found the notes, and he'd push himself to stay there. Now he just slides along. On the last album he wasn't close enough to most of the notes to hit them in the ass with a double handful of rock salt. And his playing is sloppy as hell. He got himself famous and quit trying. That burns me. There are too many people working too damned hard for him to get away with that crap."

"Like you?"

"Like me and a lot of others. This business uses talent like paper. Most of it is wasted. There are all sorts of talented people out there who are never going to get anywhere. And here's old Tommy just sliding by."

"Why'd you work so hard with him?"

"He was good. I could tell that. And he wanted it so bad. I needed a guitar player, and he was on the way to being one. I figured I could teach him right. And I liked him. He was a good kid. And old Eldon Morton. He took a chance on me. I figured I owed for that. One day when I needed a picker, there he was. He wasn't a hell of a lot better than a hundred, five hundred, kids trying to break in. I mean, he could play. Damn, he was quicker than a hiccup, but he didn't know the instrument very well. Neither did I when I started. I taught him the way others taught me. He sang flat, so I worked with him. I made him sing with me. I made him reach for the notes until he got them. And he worked. He worked like the devil."

"But people taught you, and then you moved on. You got famous. Eldon Morton never got famous."

"Right. But I never turned my back on them. I mean, people move on. That's the way it works. But you don't forget where you came from. Tommy never looked back. He acts like he did it all himself. Hell, I don't want to talk about this anymore. Anyway, I'm opening for him in Phoenix."

"Well, I don't know what to say. Good luck, I guess."

"Why don't you say you're coming back tonight?"

"I'd like to. Believe me I would. But I have a child. I've left him with someone two nights in a row now."

"How about your ex?"

"My ex doesn't have anything to do with him. Besides, that's not really the problem. I don't think you should go running around, shut-

tling your kid from house to house. I need to spend some time with
him."

"I'd really like you to come back. This is my last night here."

"I want to, Bad. I really do. Let me see what I can do. Maybe
Barbara can keep him just one more night. I don't know. Can I call
you?"

"Please. Please call."

She calls. It is three o'clock in the afternoon. He is watching
television. But he can't get interested. He turns up the sound. In a
courtroom, two grown men argue over cookies. "What I ordered,"
one man explains, "was four gross of three-and-one-half-inch-diame-
ter oatmeal cookies." Bad gets up and turns off the sound. The phone
rings.

"Bad, listen. I'm really sorry. I have to stay home tonight."

"This is my last night. I'm in Las Cruces tomorrow night."

"I know. I know. I really want to. It's my son. I really have to stay
home with my son. You understand that, don't you?"

"Sure, darlin', I understand."

"No, no, of course you don't. I just can't go off and leave him again.
I have to think of him before me, before us. I just can't."

"Look. Do you really want to see me?"

"Yes, Bad. Yes, I do."

"Can I come over there? I don't get off until one-thirty. He'll be
in bed."

There is a long pause at the other end. "You can't stay. I mean,
you have to be gone before seven."

"I can do that. I can't do it pretty or graceful, but I can do it."

"O.K. Come on over."

"How do I get there?"

"Well, when you leave the motel, turn right and go about a mile
and get back on the interstate, then it's about three miles. . . ."

"Is this north or south?"

"It's north, for about three miles, maybe more. Oh hell. I'll sneak
out and come and get you. Will you be ready at one-thirty?"

"I'll be ready."

"Promise me. I've never left him alone."

"I'll be ready. I promise."

Chapter Six

The Saturday house is not as good as the Friday house, but it's crowded and the audience responds. He sticks to the play list, working his way through it. He fights the feeling he should hurry this up. The band isn't a new treat anymore. He has become comfortable with them. He plays easily and concentrates on singing. They remain steady behind him, and there are no surprises. It is a work night, the way it is supposed to be.

At the break, Wesley Barnes comes up to him. "I want to thank you," he says, "for helping Jean out. She's a real nice girl. I mean, she's not a girl anymore. But she's real nice. She hasn't had an easy time of it. Her divorce, the boy, and all. But she's solid as a rock. I think the world of her. She's just real nice, you know?"

Bad looks at him, unsure what this means. "She is real nice," he says. "You're right to be proud of her. She's just real nice."

Wesley gives him a big smile, like he has just got something settled, something that was gnawing on him. There are little drops of sweat on the top of his head.

"And," Bad says, "thank you. For playing with me. You're real fine. Better than a lot of professionals I've played with. I wish I had a road band again. I'd like to have you with me. This is the most fun I've had in years. You, and the rest of the boys, you're all real good."

"We just do it for fun."

"That's the way it's supposed to be. It usually isn't, but it's supposed to be. You all have made it fun for me. God, I hope I get to come back and play with you again sometime."

Wesley Barnes grins. "Yes. Yes, that would be fine. We'd like that."

"You all just keep having fun."

By the end of the last set she is not there. By the end of the encore of "Slow Boat" she is not there. He packs up and says his goodbyes to the band, the barmaids and the manager. As he is loading up, Rocky Parker comes up behind him and hands him a picture. It is an eight-by-ten, an old publicity still. Bad remembers the picture. It must have been '63 or '64. In the picture he is wearing a blue suit with silver sequins and a white scarf knotted at his throat. He has a Stetson 4X beaver pushed back on his head. He is holding the Guild archtop he lost years ago. He remembers. It was a sweet guitar.

"This is kind of embarrassing," Rocky says, "but would you sign this for me?"

"To Rocky and Sureshot," Bad writes, "Bad's Boys in Santa Fe. With my thanks, Bad."

"I really appreciate it," Rocky says. "I've always been a big fan."

"Tell you what, old buddy, now I'm one of yours."

He has been sitting in the van, smoking, lighting them off the butts, hoping no one notices he is still sitting in the parking lot like he has nowhere to go and nothing to do. The bar is closed and he needs a drink. He considers going back to the room for his bottle, but he is afraid he'll miss her. It is a quarter of two when she finally pulls into the parking lot.

"I'm sorry," she says, "I was out of gas. You know how hard it is to find a gas station at one o'clock?"

"I get off work at one o'clock. I know how hard it is to find everything at one o'clock. I'm just glad you found me."

*   *   *

She knows how to drive with someone following her. She slows to make sure they will both make the lights, and he stays right with her. They wind through a complex of apartments, twenty or thirty two-story buildings with six or eight apartments in each.

"Sweet Jesus," he says when they are inside her apartment. "You read all of these books?"

"Most of them. I was an English major in college. I love to read. We'll have to keep quiet. I don't have men over. I'm not going to have him wake up in the morning and find a stranger in his house."

"Did you know I have a boy, too? He's twenty-four. Name is Steven. He lives in Los Angeles."

"You get to see him very often?"

"No. Marge took him when he was four. I never got her tracked down. Here, look at this . . ." He takes a gold money clip from his pocket. "This is his. I bought it for his eighteenth birthday. Somehow I figured I could send it to him. But I never knew where he lived. I carry it with me. Someday I might run into him. I want him to have it."

"You've never heard from him in twenty years?"

"Not once. His mother took off and left. I tracked her down to L.A. Then, I don't know. I just couldn't figure she was really mad enough to try so hard to get away from me. I figured she'd cool off and call me. You know, want alimony or something. I never heard from either of them again. But kids, you know, they're all trying to find their mothers and fathers these days. I keep hoping he's going to find me."

"Why Steven?"

"It's a real name. I wanted him to have a regular name. One that wouldn't embarrass him like mine did me."

"I don't know your name. Goddamn. I don't believe it. I don't know your name."

"Otis. Otis Arthur Blake. Otis Arthur Blake, Junior, as a matter of fact. I loved my daddy, I really did. But ain't that a damned awful thing to do to your own kid? I sure as hell wasn't about to do it to mine."

She is trying to keep a straight face. "I don't know," she says. "I mean, it was your father's name. That's nice. Oh hell. You're right, Otis Arthur is a damned awful name."

"Worse. At home they all called me Otie. Soon as I left, I became Art. That lasted a couple of months, then I was Bad."

"I promise," she says, "I'll never call you Otie."

"We'll get along just fine."

On top of the television is a framed color portrait of a boy about three or four. "This is him?"

"Daniel Rawlings Craddock. Buddy."

"Fine-looking boy. Fine-looking mother."

"How about you and that fine-looking mother going into the other room? I hate to bring this up, but you've got to be out of here by sunup."

He had a fiddle player, Cletus Young, who said he played his fiddle like a woman's body. That was only one sign Cletus was a jerk. But there's something about love that's like music. It's a way that your body begins something and then becomes what it does. Their love-making, still a little strange, a little nervous, is like playing. It's the counterpoint of single note and chord. It's the tonic, dominant, sub-dominant, and the sudden ascent to relative minor. Their bodies are the same chords played an octave apart, the movement familiar from hundreds of times before, but still unexpected. Pleasing in the familiar strangeness of it all. He has the feeling, tangled into her, of being where he belongs, like a progression that takes an unexpected turn and ends up not where he thinks it is going but where it has to go, as if he has known, without knowing he did.

He dreams of water. He pumps it up from the well in Judah, pushing the pump handle in long, steady strokes. The water comes into his cup, copper green, then clears. He draws a drink from the chrome faucet. In the glass, the water is copper green. It clears from the bottom. He considers trying another faucet, though he doesn't know where the next one is, only that the water will come out copper green and then clear from the bottom up.

It is barely light. He doesn't know what time it is. There is a clock on the dresser, but it is several feet away, and he doesn't have his glasses. Jean is asleep beside him, her hands in fists, curled under her chin. They have, he suspects, only a little time. He moves his hand down her back, across her hip and down her thigh. She stirs and turns away, moving her back into him. He is working on getting the angle, when something smacks against his butt.

"Read?" a voice asks.

He rolls over, pulling the sheet over himself. Next to the bed is a small boy, wearing only a pair of baggy briefs. In his left hand he holds a blue bowl made of soft plastic. Milk and Cheerios slosh over the edge. In his right hand he holds a thin paper book by its cover. He smacks the book against Bad's leg. "Read," he says.

"Read?"

"Read."

"Well, old buddy," he says, trying to regain his composure, "what's your name?" He shakes Jean's shoulder, trying to wake her.

"Buddy."

"That's right. What's your name?"

"Buddy."

"O.K., little buddy, you want to watch TV or something?"

"Read?"

"I'm not too good at reading. You sure you don't want to watch TV?"

"What's your name?"

"Bad. What's yours?"

"No. Buddy."

"Right. Buddies." He looks over to Jean, then back to Buddy, holding his finger to his lips. She doesn't wake.

Buddy turns and walks out of the room. He stops at the door. "Read?"

By the time he finds his glasses and clothes, Jean has stirred awake. "What time is it?"

"Early," he says. "Stay in bed. I'll take care of myself."

In the living room, he stops at the sofa to pull on his socks and boots. Buddy watches from around the corner of the breakfast bar. Bad pats the sofa cushion next to him. Buddy walks slowly over, sits down next to him and hands him the book. *Bernie and the Firetruck.*

When Jean comes into the room in her robe, Buddy is on Bad's lap, explaining the story of Bernie and the Firetruck to him. Bad looks up at Jean. "Sorry, I guess we kind of overslept. You care for some breakfast?"

Her expression is one he can't quite read. "Buddy," she says, "this is Bad. Bad, this is Buddy."

"No," Buddy says. "Buddies."

"Let's go make your mom breakfast."

While she is in the bathroom, he finds most of the ingredients he needs. Buddy hands him spoons and packages. He is almost done, when he realizes he is missing one ingredient. He walks to the bathroom door. "Where do you keep the cream of tartar?"

"I don't have any. What the hell do you want cream of tartar for?"

"Biscuits. Don't you use cream of tartar in your biscuits?"

"I don't make biscuits."

"And here I thought you were such a good woman."

They eat biscuits and eggs while Buddy plays on the living room floor. "That's a real nice boy you got."

"I know. He likes you, that's for sure. He's not around men all that much. I'm kind of surprised."

"Doesn't he spend time with your ex?"

She shakes her head and takes another biscuit. "Buddy's not his. I had him two years after the divorce." She waits for a response, gets none, and goes on. "You get older, you get wiser, but you still make mistakes. Only sometimes mistakes don't turn out that way."

"Mine usually do. But I know what you mean. He's a good boy. Good mom."

"Good biscuits."

It is five hours due south on I-25 to Las Cruces. Past Albuquerque, the heat builds steadily. He sweats and drives, his heart beating evenly and slowly. He has tonight in Las Cruces and then it is on to Arizona, and Phoenix.

Between sets, he stands at the bar and pumps hands. Yes, yes, he says, that's just wonderful. Tommy's like my own son, he says to a couple who want to know what Tommy is like.

"How about 'Let's Get Drunk and Screw'?" This from a young woman who has appeared in front of him. She is in her early twenties, thin and blond, in tight jeans and a cotton chemise top that shows her nipples. She wears a tooled belt with a large silver buckle. He knows the belt is carved in back, "Debbie" or "Robin." Debbie, he decides. She has a longneck in one hand and a cigarette in the other. She is also chewing gum.

"Pardon?"

" 'Let's Get Drunk and Screw,' you do it?"

"The song or the mistake?"

"The song. Mostly."

"I know it. I've done it. I don't do it anymore."

84

"The song or the mistake?" She cocks her head and takes a drag on the cigarette, closing one eye. Bad watches the shirt tighten across her breasts.

She smiles and tilts her head in the other direction, her eye still closed, though the smoke is more in his face than hers now. "It ain't always a mistake, you know."

"I sure as hell used to believe that. Every once in a while I can still convince myself of it. Mostly it's a mistake, though."

"Have it your way," she says, shrugging her shoulders. " 'The Wrangler of Love,' huh?"

"I made a whole bunch of mistakes in my life, darlin'. That's why I know so much about them."

She shakes her head and turns away. The back of her belt reads "Jackie."

He's made enough mistakes in his life, he thinks, to know about all there is to know about them. He's also made enough to know that he hasn't made one for a long time now.

He is on I-10, fifty miles out of Tucson, watching a blue Pontiac that he has been following for four or five miles. It is a late sixties model, with Georgia plates and a broken left taillight. There are two people in the front seat, a man and a woman. For miles the woman has been moving closer to the man. Occasionally their heads merge and seem to become one. Then she will pull back, nuzzle, and begin the process again.

What interests Bad is that now her head has disappeared completely. This can mean only one thing, he thinks. Actually, it can mean any number of things, but only one is worth considering at the moment. It is hot and the road is threatening never to end. He pushes down the accelerator, pulling up closer to the Pontiac. He can see the man's head clearly now. He has brown hair, but not a lot of it. This pleases Bad. He cannot see the woman. He signals and pulls into the right lane, where he can get a better look.

He remembers a night in Minnesota, 1959 or 1960. He let the rest of the band have the bus and he and the new backup singer rode alone in a rented De Soto, on ahead of the bus into blackness that turned into snow. He drove with one hand, trying to coax her head into his lap with the other. Both of them were giggling, lustful, too drunk to be afraid of snow and slick roads, too happy to quit drinking. When the bus finally caught up with them and pulled the De Soto from the

85

snowbank where Bad had driven it, both he and Marge were so deep in sleep they had to be helped onto the bus.

When he pulls up even with the Pontiac, he can see the woman's foot resting on the window frame and the bunch of her shoulder on the front seat. He pulls up a little to see if he can get a better angle on the couple, when the opening bars of "Slow Boat" come whining out of the radio speaker. He has never grown tired of hearing the song come at him from a car radio or, less often, from the jukebox of a honky-tonk. Being caught by surprise by the song is like letting memories come at him shotgun. The song has been part of his life —on the worst days, his whole life—for twenty-five years.

Because he has already been thinking of Marge, he gets a twinge, a memory of him and Marge in L.A. in 1960. Twelve bars into the song, he is driving his new Cadillac convertible around the twists of Mulholland Drive in the middle of a radiant afternoon, with his wife beside him. "Slow Boat" is on the radio, and he turns it up, letting the music ricochet off retaining walls that line the road, suddenly the most intensely beautiful sight he has ever seen. The air is clear and dry in the afternoon sun. Plants atop the retaining wall burn with color. "Slow Boat" has been to number one on *Billboard*'s country chart, has stayed there nine straight weeks and now is off but still getting decent airplay. He cannot write a bad song, and he has corrected, in this second marriage, the mistakes of his first. He doesn't get tongue-tied anymore when he has to talk to men who wear suits and neckties. In short, he has stopped being a jerk.

He is now half a car length ahead of the Pontiac, angling the outside mirror so he can see into the car's front seat, and singing along with himself on the radio. He has a better view now, but he still can't decide whether he is watching sex or nausea. When he decides that he really doesn't care anymore, and pulls up another car length ahead of the Pontiac, the DJ announces that they have been listening to "Slow Boat" by "the late Mr. Bad Blake, one of the great ones." He slows down, and he can feel the sweat soaking his shirt against the vinyl of the seat. In the rearview mirror, his face is fish-belly white. He begins to look for a place to stop and get a drink. The blue Pontiac moves past him on the left. The woman is sitting upright now, and as the car passes, the driver gives Bad the O.K. sign, finger to thumb. Bad reaches for a cigarette. Here he is, sweating his way through a state where they think he is dead, on his way to be an opening act for Tommy Sweet. Yeah, I know, buddy, he thinks, ain't none of us ever stop being jerks.

*   *   *

His drink wavers in his hand, rattling the ice. He is in a tiny bar just outside Tucson, a square stucco building that stinks of piss and disinfectant. "Would you like to contribute to my next dance?" a woman in a transparent negligee asks. He shakes his head.

"You want to see, you want to pay," she says.

"Darlin', the only thing I want to see is the bottom of this glass, and the bottom of the next one, too."

"Fuck you."

"Better not, darlin', I'm a dead man."

Chapter Seven

Chapter
Seven

In Phoenix, the traffic begins to slow and stop. There is a rhythm to traffic that he loves. On the open road, it unfolds and plays slowly, gracefully. In the city, the tempo quickens, but it begins a series of variations, off the beat, an irregular pattern but still a pattern that can be followed. He has lost his itinerary and instructions. He exits the freeway and stops at a Shell station for directions, gets back on the freeway and heads north.

He exits on McDowell, heads east to Nineteenth. There is the sign. "Veterans Memorial Coliseum. August 29. Tommy Sweet. / Special Guest, Bad Blake." Jack, you cocksucker, thank you.

It takes him twice around the perimeter before he finds the one gate that is open. He pulls the van in, up to where two tractor trailers sit next to the coliseum. "Tommy Sweet" is written in script on the sides of both trailers. Beyond the trailers in the lot is a Silver Eagle bus. "Tommy Sweet" is also across the side of the bus. Below that, "Lovin' You."

At the rear door of the coliseum, a security cop lounges in a lawn chair. "Howdy," Bad says. "Bad Blake." The cop looks up, mirroring Bad in his glasses, two Bad Blakes grinning down.

"You got a stage pass?" the cop asks.

"Hell no. I just got here. I'm Bad Blake."

"I can't let you beyond this point without a pass."

"Get me a pass. I'm on the show."

"I just check passes. You're supposed to have one."

"Get Tommy, then."

"No sir. I can't do that."

"The hell." He starts to move past the guard and into the coliseum.

"I'm sorry, sir." The guard puts his hand on his gun. "You don't move past this point without a pass."

Bad goes back to the van, looks for his notes in the glove compartment, until a vague memory stirs. He goes back to the cop. "You know Ralphie?"

"Yessir."

"You go find Ralphie. You tell him Bad Blake is here. Then you tell him Bad Blake is waiting five more minutes, then he is out of here. Then you better go buy yourself a newspaper and start reading the want ads, because, buddy, your job is over here."

The cop scowls, gets up and walks inside the coliseum. Bad follows. "You wait here," the cop says. Inside it is dark and cool. He hears the cop's footsteps echo off the concrete. In the distance he can see stage lights and spots being turned off and on. The cop comes back. "Ralphie will be right here."

Bad takes a cigarette from his pocket. The cop offers him a light.

"This is my job," the cop says. "You understand that. No one gets in without a pass. No one ever gets hassled when I work a show."

"Yeah, we all got jobs."

"They should have sent you a pass. That's their job. I just make sure no one gets in without one."

"Yeah. Right."

"I work all kinds of shows here. I like these country shows. You guys are all right. Willie Nelson, he slipped me a fifty-dollar tip two years ago. I hate those damn rock-and-roll shows. All a bunch of stuck-up little shits, you know? Treat you like dirt. And then all those little girls around here. Hell, I don't let them in. I got a girl of my own. How's some guy going to feel, his daughter running around in the middle of the night, trying to put out for some faggot in pink pants and mascara? God, it makes me sick."

"Yeah. Hell of a thing. Any of those girls come around looking for me, let 'em in. I don't wear mascara."

"And the Ice Capades. I bet every one of them is queer. And some of those girls in the show. Jesus Christ. And it's all wasted on a bunch of queers in tight pants. Oh, I get them all, believe you me."

"Bad Blake. Good to meet you." A little man in jeans and red satin jacket shakes Bad's hand. He is wearing a wireless headset with earphones and a pencil-thin mike. "Ralph Martin. I'm with Tommy. Call me Ralphie. We expected you two hours ago. You have trouble?"

"Long trip. I left Las Cruces at five this morning. Played last night. Car trouble in Tucson."

"Shit. You're tired, then. Listen, Jack Greene's got you set up at the Holiday Inn right down the road here. Soon as we're done, I'll have someone take you over. We're in sound check right now, so things won't be too long. Come on up, take a look around."

"I got a band here?"

"Yeah, yeah. They showed up about eleven. We're running a little late, you know. All the union guys trying to run into the double bubble here. Your guys are downstairs, I'll take you down in just a minute. I think they're having lunch. You hungry?"

"Well, now that you mention it."

"We got the food downstairs. Just a minute. Come on up on the stage. And here. Put this on." He takes a cloth patch and sticks it to the leg of Bad's jeans—"Tommy Sweet, Lovin' You."

They climb up ten wooden stairs, onto the stage. Roadies in undershirts are busy taping wires to the stage. At both ends of the stage, amps are stacked—Altecs, Fenders and Marshalls. At the back of the stage is a Rogers drum kit with double bass and two synthesized drums. At the far end is a Baldwin grand piano. Around the stage are stacked blue Anvil crates on casters. Stenciled on the sides is "Tommy Sweet." From above, beyond the basketball scoreboard in the middle of the arena, baby spots sweep across the floor. "Bear," Ralphie says into his microphone, "stage, please." Then, to Bad, "Bear handles our sound, he'll help you set up."

Bad looks out across the arena. There are two tiers of seats, which run in a horseshoe from the stage to about a hundred yards back. On the floor, plywood covering the basketball court, chairs are set up in two sections all the way back to the first tier of permanents. "How are tickets?"

"Not bad. No sellout, but we were at ninety-three at noon. Maybe ninety-six or ninety-seven by showtime. It's not great, but it's O.K. We're running radio spots until seven tonight."

Sweet Jesus. Last night in Las Cruces, they estimated the house at one-fifty. He looks back out at the seats. Ninety-six or ninety-seven hundred people here tonight. "Where's Tommy?"

"Back at the hotel. He'll come in for final check about five-thirty and then he'll head back to the hotel until showtime. He said he's anxious to see you. Maybe he'll be by early."

A huge, fat man in a sleeveless cowboy shirt moves across the stage toward them. "What's up, man?"

"Bear, this is Bad Blake. You'll need to get him set up. How's this going?"

"Fucked up the butt, man. We got buzz on channel eight we can't get out and monitor three's dead. The usual. Fucked right up the butt. How you doin', man? What's your equipment like?"

"Roland Cube."

"That's it? A Roland Cube? Well, that ain't going to bounce off the back wall. No sweat. We'll run you through one of these. You got a preference—Marshall, Fender? Like it don't matter. Those boys with you got a god-awful mix of stuff—Mesas, Peaveys, heavy rock-and-roll shit. Suit yourself."

"I like my Roland."

"Well, that's no sweat, either. I'll mike it through the PA. What else you need?"

"Just time to rehearse."

"Give me thirty minutes to get this stuff untangled, and come on up. Where's your stuff?"

"Parking lot. Black Dodge van."

"Give me the keys. I'll take care of it. Go on downstairs and chow down. I'll call you when we're clear up here."

On their way down the stairs, Ralphie runs through the program. "You go on at eight-fifteen. You got forty-five minutes. Stay on that. I'll be stage left and I'll give you your time remaining. You can't run over more than three minutes. Tommy goes on at nine-thirty. Tommy's off at eleven-thirty. We're torn down and out of here by one-thirty. May be some party at the hotel around two or so. You're welcome." They are on a winding corridor that leads past the locker room. "This is your dressing room. Tommy's is the next one down."

When he opens the door, Bad walks into a room that looks like a bus station john, white tile floor and wall, mirrors and sinks along the length of one wall. Beyond the sinks, five men sit on folding chairs, eating and drinking. "Maverick," Ralphie says, "your backup." Bad walks over and introduces himself. Beyond the band, on the shelf in front of the mirror, are four plates of cold cuts, cheese, bread and relishes, cans of beer, bottles of wine, soft drinks, glasses, ice, and a case of Jack Daniel's with a note. "Save some for me. Tommy."

While they eat, Bad goes over the play list with Maverick. He has cut three sets down to one, keeping to big stuff, keeping it simple. He has a drummer, bass player, two guitars and pedal steel. He would like to keep the stuff he tried in Santa Fe, but they have two hours onstage before they play before ninety-seven hundred people. The band knows most of the songs by sight, and have "Slow Boat," "Faded Love," "I Love You (A Thousand Ways)," "Love Came and Got Me" in their repertoire. What they don't know, they are intelligent enough to ask about.

"What we are doing here," Bad tells them, "is opening. It's Tommy's show. We go out, we play our forty-five minutes straight. We don't get cute or fancy. We do our work, nothing more."

"Jesus, Lord," Ray, the bass player, says when they get on the stage. "This place is about twice as big from down here as from up there."

"You ever played an arena before?"

"Hell no. We played five hundred at a barbecue once."

"Not a hell of a lot of difference," Bad tells him, "except the sound. It's going to crunch you when you first hear it. Get used to it, and remember, it won't be as loud when there are people here."

The band is competent enough. The guitars can't resist moving up to the front of the stage to try rock-and-roll licks. Bad lets them go. Tonight they will stand stone still behind him.

"Bear," he says into the microphone, "bring up number one mike, the bass, and tone down the guitars."

"Mix is good," a voice responds.

"Set it the way I tell you, and leave it."

"I've got a good read out here. Your mix is fine. Trust me."

95

"Bear, I'm an old man. I get grumpy. Bring up the lead mike, the bass, set the guitars down, and humor me."

"You want one of us to go there and check the mix?" Nick the rhythm guitar player asks.

"We're going to get a shit mix," Bad tells him. "Opening acts always do. One of the sound man's jobs is to fuck up the opening mix. It makes the headline act sound that much better. We can send the whole band out there. It won't make a hell of a difference. What we're doing here is negotiating just how bad a mix we're getting."

"You've got another fifty minutes of stage time," Bear says.

"We're going to be on this stage until the mix is where I want it. Give me my mix or we may rehearse right through Tommy's first set."

When he has pushed Bear as far as he thinks he is willing to go, Bad moves them through the rest of the play list, and comes back and works the rough edges off "Slow Boat" and "Cheatin' Night Tonight."

"You're off in five minutes," Bear calls.

"Fifteen," Bad responds, and takes the band through three more numbers. He is off in fifteen minutes. He can't let the sound man push him, or the sound man will run the show. On the other hand, he can't throw the sound man too far off, or the mix will sound like the track to an auto wreck.

"Sounds good, Mr. Blake."

"I like the mix, Bear. I appreciate it."

"What do you think?" he asks Ron, the pedal steel.

"Sounds good. Simple enough. We can handle it."

Just wait, Bad thinks, until you walk out here and realize that there are nearly ten thousand people in those seats. Then you handle it.

"I'll drive you to the hotel now," Ralphie says. "I'll send someone by at seven to pick you up." Then, to the band, "You need to be in the dressing room at seven-fifteen. Your instruments will be onstage. They'll be tuned for you."

"No," Bad says. "Have them down here. We'll tune ourselves."

"We'll tune them on the scope. We'll have them under the lights so they'll stay in tune."

"I'll tune. You can take them up fifteen minutes before, but we tune to me."

Ralphie turns and walks away. Bad breaks open the case and takes

96

a bottle out for the hotel. A couple of the guys take them, too. "Hold it," Bad says. "You're welcome to the booze. That's no problem. But now you're working for me. You be real careful with that stuff. Anyone shows up drunk, I'm personally kicking his ass up between his ears."

At the hotel, there is a message for him. "Call me, #647, Tommy." Bad folds the note and puts it in his pocket. In his room, he undresses and climbs onto the bed. He needs an hour or two of sleep. His stomach is churning, and his heart is pounding like an engine about to throw a rod.

It is 1951, in Lexington, Kentucky. He is sitting in the bus with the rest of the Kentucky Bluebirds, waiting. Out the window, beyond the fence, he can see cars pulling in, people milling around. It is over two hours to showtime, but they are lining up outside the armory, waiting for Hank Williams.

He has seen Williams twice before. Once in Louisville, once in Ohio after driving all night with Leon, just for a chance to see Hank, to watch him work, to see him in person. Tonight he is opening with the Bluebirds for Hank Williams. He is going to walk onto the same stage Hank Williams will walk onto. He is going to play for the same people Hank Williams is going to sing for.

He keeps looking out the window. Beyond the fence are only cars and people. He can see only a few yards down the road, to where it curves behind the trees. He really doesn't know what he expects to see—another bus, a procession of Cadillacs, a golden cloud. "You nervous?" Leon asks him. No, he lies, no, he is not nervous. It's another date in Kentucky. He has been playing them for nearly two years now. What he wants to know is whether Hank is nervous about having to follow him.

They play their first set, leave the stage, and ten minutes later are back on for another set. Hank is still not here. They play nearly every song they know and repeat a couple. They have been playing for nearly two hours when the word comes, "Hank is here."

He is off the stage, putting his guitar in the case, when Hank Williams walks past him, nearly as tall as he is, but thin as a guitar string, smoking a cigar that seems as thick as his arm. He is wearing a white suit decorated with quarter notes up the leg and down the arms. And he is wearing the fanciest pair of black-and-white boots Bad

97

has ever seen. Bad watches Hank move up behind the stage for the intro, grind out the cigar, and take off his hat and wipe the sweat from his head. Bad is stunned. Hank Williams is going bald.

After he is done, Hank moves around backstage, smoking his cigar and swigging on a bottle of bourbon. He is not very old, not out of his twenties yet, but he is balding and he looks drawn and weary, even while he ambles through the backstage crush, shaking hands and chatting, smiling all the time. Hank stops and chats with Eldon, and then moves through the other members of the band. Bad sticks out his hand and Williams takes it. "I heard you. You can pick some guitar, Slim." He holds out the bottle. "Want a slug?"

Chapter Eight

When the knock comes at the door, he is between sleep and waking, unsure what time it is. He finds his glasses, but there is no clock in the room. It must be, he figures, time to leave for the coliseum. He gets out of the bed and gets dressed, his heart heaving and skipping beats. "I'll be right there."

"Hurry up, goddamn it, we run a tight ship here."

Goddamned efficient little shit. Runs a show like a fucking space mission. He runs a comb through his hair and opens the door.

"I got booze, you got ice?" Tommy says, holding up a bottle.

"You son-of-a-bitch."

"I always admired that in you, Bad. You always know the right thing to say. How the hell are you?"

"Worse."

"That's about right, I guess. Can I come in?"

Bad steps aside and lets Tommy into the room. Tommy holds up the bottle. "I could use some ice."

"None here. Try room service."

Tommy plops down in a chair next to the bed, where he rests his feet. His boots are made of thin strips of leather, sewn together so they form a series of V's pointing down to the toes. Bad estimates six hundred bucks, maybe seven. His jeans are crisp and new, his starched white shirt is monogrammed at the pocket. On his right hand he has a diamond ring in the shape of Texas. "I can do without ice," he says, "but a glass would help. A couple of them."

Bad finds glasses in the bathroom, brings them in and sets them down on the dresser. Tommy pours three fingers of Wild Turkey in each one.

"You give up on the Southern Comfort?"

"I still drink it onstage. It's good for the throat."

"So they tell me. Damn stuff was always too sweet for me."

"When I started drinking, it was the only thing I could choke down. I didn't like it much, either. But hell, if you're one of Bad's Boys, you got to be able to put away the whiskey. Hell, those were good times, weren't they, Bad?"

"Yeah. We had some good times. You remember Bob Glover? I ran into him a couple days ago in New Mexico."

"Bob Glover. Bob Glover. Oh, hell yes, I remember Bob. Remember, one night in Arkansas, he had some girl in his room, and you started banging on the door, screaming like you were her husband. And I was yelling, 'Don't shoot, please don't shoot our drummer.' "

"No. That was Will Samuels."

"Will Samuels, hell yes. We had him so scared he crawled out the bathroom window bare-assed. Who the hell is Bob Glover?"

"Bass player. About sixty, sixty-one. Came over from Lee Stoner's group."

"Yeah, maybe I remember him. Kind of a quiet guy."

"He's a grandfather."

"You don't say. You remember Kelly, my little girl? She's seventeen now. Going to college next year."

"I'll be damned." Bad takes a long drink and lights up a cigarette.

"Bad. It's good to see you again. I'm really glad you agreed to do this for me. It'll be great to be working together again."

"I need the money. If it wasn't this, I'd be playing Benson, Arizona, tonight."

"Benson? Where's that?"

"Real damn close to Tombstone."

"Listen, you remember that time we broke down in the middle of west Texas? Two hundred miles from El Paso? We sat out there all goddamned day waiting for the wrecker while Ted Randolph sat in some bar getting shit-faced. It must have been a hundred and ten out there. I thought old Paul was going to die. Why the hell was Ted at the bar?"

"The guy who owned the wrecker was at lunch. Ted went to get a drink. He kept on drinking. Is that why you wear the ring?"

Tommy looks at the ring on his finger. "Ain't that a bitch? You ever try to buy a diamond ring in the shape of Kansas?"

"Kansas is square."

"See what I mean? Nobody knows what the hell it looks like."

"So how's the tour going?"

"It's O.K. Fifty dates in two months. It's a grind, but it'll pay for Kelly's college, a few other things. How about yours?"

"I'm out for a month. Six states. I'll be off next week."

"Pickup bands?"

"Yeah."

"Jesus, that's a ball buster. Hell, we should have gotten together earlier. We could have done this whole tour together."

"We tried that once. It didn't work."

"Yeah. I know. The *Memories* tour. Hell, there were just too many things going on. I had that movie shooting in Mexico, and Jill wanted me to spend some time at home. I was on the road almost all that year. I wanted to do it. It would have been a hell of a tour."

"Yeah. A hell of a tour."

"Oh, come on, Bad. I'm sorry. It just didn't work out. I was trying to keep my marriage together. Don't hold that against me."

"I got a career, too. And I had a marriage or two I wanted to keep together."

"Goddamn it. You gave me my start. I remember that, Bad. You taught me most of what I know that's worth knowing. O.K.? I haven't forgotten any of that. But goddamn it, I have a life to live, too."

"Yeah. Well, hell. Those are the goddamned ugliest boots I ever saw in my life."

"You ever see a boa constrictor? Ugly damn snake. Ugly damn boots."

"Salesman threaten to shoot your dog?"

"Kind of like the idea of wearing snakes on my feet. Besides that, they were expensive. Real expensive. I like that. When I spend my money, it means that no one else is spending it."

"So why the hell won't you do another album?"

"Hold up. I never said I wouldn't. J.M.I. doesn't think it's the right time to do another duet."

"I think it is."

"You might be right. But over at J.M.I., marketing says it's the wrong time. Hell, they got those guys over there making all this money, my money, and they call the plays. They want a couple more solos, then we can do a duet. You got first shot. I already told them that."

"I don't have a lot more time. I need some money now."

"Look, even if we go to the studio—say I front the money to cut the album—they won't release it. They'll sit on it until they think it's right. You won't make any money with tape sitting in the vault."

"Shit, Tommy. I'm fifty-six years old. My career isn't going anywhere. I need something to get it moving again. I can't get a solo album. I need this. Goddamn it, I really need this."

"I hear you, Bad. I really hear you. But I can't get them to budge on this one. There is a way you can make some money, though."

"Which is?"

"Songs. I need some songs. I'm supposed to be in the studio in two months for a solo album. I don't have new material, and the stuff I've been hearing is just crap. Give me some new songs. I'll deal straight with you. You publish and I'll give you three cents for the mechanical rights, the others on line, above going rate. I've been moving one or two million on every album. And I'd take up to five songs."

"I haven't written a new song in three years."

"Think about it. I need some material. I want some from you. Jesus, you write some of the best material around."

"I used to."

"I tell you what. If you can get me some new songs, and I take them, we'll release at least one as a single. I can guarantee that."

"Look, like I told you, I don't have any new songs."

"Write me some. I don't have to be in the studio until October. You've got a couple of months."

"I'm not a songwriter anymore. I haven't been in years. It doesn't matter what kind of figures you come up with. You're really not offering me anything. I'm a singer and a picker. We can do an album, but I can't write you any songs."

"Do it, Bad. You're not the only one who's hurting. I could really use a hit right now. I haven't put a single to the top in over a year."

"Scary, isn't it?"

"What?"

"Staring at nothing. You got any of that whiskey left?"

"Oh hell, it's just a little dry spell. But yeah, it gets worrisome."

"It gets to be a whole lot of fun later on."

Bad's into his third drink when the phone rings.

"Mr. Blake, it's Brenda. I have a message from Mr. Greene."

"If he wants to know if I'm here, tell him I am."

"No. He wants you to know he's sent you five boxes of product and he's cleared it with Sweet Productions so you can sell them at the concert."

"Sell? What the hell are you talking about?"

"He's bought five hundred units of *Memories* from J.M.I. at two dollars. He says you're supposed to sell them for five dollars each."

"What the hell is going on? I don't sell anything. I sing. I play. I don't sell my goddamned records at concerts."

"Mr. Blake, all I have is this message. He wants three dollars a unit. You're to keep the rest."

"Son-of-a-bitch. Let me talk to him."

"He's out of town. On the Coast. He just left this message for you."

"That motherfucking prick. Where is he? Get him for me."

"He's not here, Mr. Blake. I can't reach him. I'm sorry."

"You find him. And when you do, you tell him to get his fat ass to Phoenix and pick up his goddamn albums. Because this is where they are going to stay. You tell him that. And you tell him he's a worthless son-of-a-bitch with more nerve than brains."

"I'm just delivering the message, Mr. Blake."

"Hell, I know that, darlin'. Nothing against you. You just deliver that message back is all."

"I'll tell him. Mr. Blake, I'm sorry."

"Yeah, darlin', I know. Me, too."

Bad slams the receiver down, ringing the phone.

"That," Tommy says, "was not your basic good news."

"Fucking jackass wants me to hawk copies of *Memories* after the show."

"Well, hell, Bad, that's no problem. We got concessionaires working at all my shows. We'll just turn the records over to them. They'll sell them for you. No sweat."

"I don't sell albums at my shows."

"Well, damn it, I do. I mean, the concessionaires do. Everybody does it. How many you got?"

"I ain't got any. Jack Greene's got five hundred. And if he wants them sold, he's going to have to do it himself."

"What do you get off each one?"

"Two dollars."

"That's a thousand bucks. Hell, for a thousand bucks, I'll go sell them."

"You're welcome to them."

"Think about it. I mean, that's the business, right? Selling product? One way or another, you're selling the stuff. I got to go. It's getting on showtime. Listen, I've got all day in Phoenix tomorrow. What do you say we go play a little golf in the morning? I'm better than I used to be. Hell, I break ninety every now and again."

"I got to get back on the road early."

"That's too bad. You used to hit a good ball. I remember."

"Ain't remembering wonderful?"

The band is already there when he arrives. There is a new arrangement of food on the dressing table. The air is acrid with marijuana. Bad finds a roach in an ashtray and lights up.

"You all eaten yet? Eat some if you can, but don't overdo it. A little bit will help settle your stomachs. Have a couple of drinks, but no more. It's O.K. to be nervous. It'll go away. You get drunk, that won't go away. You blow a couple of notes early on, it doesn't make much difference, but the end of the show has to be tight."

"This is fucking living," Nick says, building a ham sandwich. "A couple more years, we're going to have shit like this every night."

"Yeah, I hope you do," Bad says, working on the roast beef. "But let's get through tonight first."

"You get this kind of stuff all the time?"

"I work clubs mostly. I get dinner and drinks."

"You work on the gate?"

"Flat fee."

"We get thirty-five percent over a guarantee of two hundred dollars."

"I travel alone. I can't check the gate. My agent sets a flat fee. I never have to deal with the money."

"What does your agent take?"

106

"Fifteen percent."

"Damn, is that worth it?"

"Agents are a pain in the butt. They're bastards, all of them. And you're damn right they're worth it. If you're going to do anything at all in the business, you better get yourself one."

"Half an hour." It's Ralphie at the door. "Anything you guys need?"

"I guess we're O.K."

"I'll be back in twenty minutes. While you're on, I'll be stage right. Any problems, let me know. Broken strings, that sort of stuff. Anything goes wrong, anything, make sure I'm the first to know."

"Let's tune them up," Bad says. He tunes his and then gives the band each string, thumb up for flat, back down for sharp. "You all remember the intro?"

"Of course," Nick says. "We've got it cold."

"Play it for me."

"Aw, for Christ sakes, we know it."

"Play it for me."

They go through the intro, the guitars and bass, the drummer tapping out the beat on the bottom of a chair. "Like I said, we know it."

"Don't come unwrapped. Things change out there. I know you know it. I want you to remember you know it."

"Ten minutes," Ralphie says. "Give me the instruments. We're doing the last stage check. Problems?"

"Ready to work."

"Good. Listen. I got your boxes of albums. Tommy told me to put them with the concessions up on the concourse. You can check with me later on tonight for an accounting, or we'll just send the receipts along to Greene and Gold, whatever you want. Let me know after the show."

"Shit."

Ralphie leads them back up the ramp toward the stage. Along the way, they pass a couple of Tommy's boys heading for the dressing room. When they make the final turn toward the stage, they can see the horseshoe of seats nearly full. The noise of the crowd is like a low grinding.

"Holy fucking shit," Nick says.

"Just breathe," Bad says, "get your breath steady. You're fine."

His own heart is thumping like a broken cam. He inhales hard and holds it.

"In ninety seconds the houselights go down," Ralphie says. "Get a good look at the stairs. There will be two guys at the side to help you up, but you got to climb yourself. Six steps, remember that. Count as you go. It's going to be dark as hell until you reach the stage."

When the lights go down, the crowd noise comes up, as if they were wired on the same switch. Noise rolls over them.

"Go," Ralphie says.

The band moves up the steps to the stage. From the bottom of the steps, Bad can see them moving slowly across the dark stage, sees the instruments being lifted. From the corner of his eye, he sees Ralphie's hand move, and the stage lights come up. Bob taps out four beats on his sticks, and the band moves into "Wildwood Flower." Two bars in, Nick misses a chord.

"Shit," Ralphie says.

"They're O.K.," Bad says, and starts up to the stage. When he moves from behind the stacked amplifiers into the clear stage, the crowd noise intensifies, and he feels his knees begin to wobble. At the edge of the clearing, he picks up his white Gretsch and moves to the center, the microphone pulling him like a beacon. When he reaches the mike, he picks his guitar cord from the stage, while Nick makes the intro: "Ladies and gentlemen, 'The Wrangler of Love,' Mr. Bad Blake."

They are running a couple of beats behind what they have rehearsed, and when they reach the chorus, Bad is not ready, and has to just count the beat into the turnaround before he can start playing. The notes come back at him through the monitor pure and crisp. At the end of the song, the applause is politely enthusiastic.

"Thank you, Phoenix, Arizona," he says. "It's real good to be here tonight. Of course, at my age, it's real good to be anywhere." Applause and a little laughter. "This is a song I had a hit on a long time ago," he says, "called 'Love Came and Got Me.' " He will announce every song, just to make sure the band doesn't get confused.

They stay with him for the whole set. They are not as sharp as Sureshot in Santa Fe, but they are steady and dependable. The steel guitar covers the ragged edges at the ends of the progression with long, sweeping wails.

They are three quarters of the way through the set, moving into

108

"Faded Love," when the crowd begins to stomp and cheer. Finally, he has struck some response in them. From the corner of his eye he can see someone moving up toward him. As he moves into the chorus, Tommy is up to the microphone with him, singing harmony.

> *I miss you, darling,*
> *More and more every day,*
> *As heaven would miss the stars above.*
> *With every heartbeat,*
> *I still think of you*
> *And remember our faded love.*

At the next verse, Tommy picks up his blue Adamas guitar and plays rhythm behind Bad. At the choruses, he moves up and sings the harmony. Halfway through the break, Bad steps back and offers the rest to Tommy, who plays it through his way, quickly hammering and pulling, trilling the final notes. He gives Bad a grin and a nod, and Bad takes it back and runs it through once more, duplicating Tommy's moves, but elaborating on them, substituting triplets at the end. They harmonize the last chorus and bring it down.

"This is the man," Tommy says, "who taught me to play that and just about everything else. I guess he can still teach, huh?" The crowd begins to cheer and Tommy steps back and waits, careful not to step on any of Bad's applause. When it starts to die down, he says, "I'll see you all in a little bit. I'm going to go back and listen to this man play."

When they have finished "Slow Boat" there is no question of a curtain call. The band unplugs and waves. "You all know," Bad says into the microphone, "that Tommy and me did an album a couple of years ago. You can't get it at the record stores anymore, but we got some copies of it up at the concession stand. I'll be up there in a little bit, if you'd like to have me sign some of them for you. Come by and say howdy. Thanks, and God bless you."

As he's leaving the stage, Ralphie grabs him. "Tommy would like you to join him in his set for 'Please Release Me' and 'Cold, Cold Heart.' I'll cue you."

"No," Bad says. "This is Tommy's show. I got records to sell."

He moves through the crush of people on the concourse easily for a bit, until heads start to turn and people move up to pat him on the back and shake his hand. By the time he reaches the concession stand, people are waiting with copies of the record in their hands. He puts on his glasses and starts signing them on people's backs. "Best Wishes, Bad Blake."

"Is Tommy going to come up and sign them, too?" a couple of people ask.

"No," Bad says. "I don't think Tommy's coming up."

When the houselights start to flash the five-minute warning, there is still a sizable crowd waiting. A few move back toward their seats. "The show is about to start," Bad says. "Why don't you all get back to your seats and enjoy it. Maybe I can see you afterwards." Thirty or forty remain, stubbornly waiting for him to sign their albums. He stays and signs even after the houselights go down and Tommy's band starts up. The sound is crisp as new beans, and as he listens, he knows Tommy has paid a lot of money for these arrangements— piano, horns, strings, as tight and methodical as Muzak.

He still has his back to the stage, signing albums, when he hears the reaction of the crowd, and then the repetitive hammering on the guitar. There is not even an introduction. He turns his head to the stage as Tommy, still in the same jeans and white shirt, with a high-crowned straw hat, begins his version of "Lost Highway."

Back in the dressing room, the band is eating and drinking, listening to Tommy's show through the intercom. From somewhere, girls have appeared, and the band is having its own little party. Bad makes his way through a couple of dancers to the bar. His case of Jack Daniel's is well broken into. He pours a glass and leans back against the mirror to watch.

"I blew that intro," Nick says. "Jesus, I'm sorry. I got out there and started shaking so hard I thought I was going to fall down."

"It's no problem. You're not the first to do it. I wasn't the first, either. Just forget it and have a good time."

"I don't think I've ever had this much fun in my life. Jesus, backing Bad Blake and Tommy Sweet on the same night."

"Yeah," Bad says, "it's a goddamned bunch of fun, isn't it?"

While the boys party, Bad eats Tommy's food and drinks Tommy's booze. He listens, through the intercom, to Tommy's show. Even through the six-inch speaker, he can tell this show is as smooth as a baby's butt. Though, my God, what a mess Tommy can make of good material. On "Bright Side," his first hit, Tommy has cluttered the song with horns and strings until it is nearly a new number. He thinks of Marge and the things she used to do with Jell-O. She put fruit and nuts in it, whipped cream and ice cream, she whipped it and chopped it in pieces. She served it in bowls, cups and glasses, but it always came out Jell-O.

"Excuse me," a red-haired girl in cowboy shirt and jeans says. "I want to get to the food here." Bad smiles and steps aside. "You were very good. I enjoyed it. A real nice show."

"Thanks, I appreciate it."

As she bends over to get at the relishes, she shows off the Tommy Sweet patch on the rear pocket of her jeans.

"You with the tour?" Bad asks.

"Local radio," she says. "I hit most of the shows. Linda Fuller."

"Bad Blake. Linda, you a DJ?"

"Advertising."

"Here for the party?"

"Mostly. Sometimes they can be pretty fun. I bring clients sometimes. It builds goodwill to let them meet a few stars. Usually it's a way to pass the time."

"The boys seem to be having a pretty good time."

She shrugs. "The real party will start after the band gets off. I'll check it out, I guess."

Over the intercom, the band stops and the crowd noise comes up. "You know when they're planning to get off?"

"Eleven-thirty."

"That'll be three, then."

"Three?"

"Curtain calls. About seven minutes each, I figure."

"You been to a few of these shows."

"It beats television, usually."

The crowd noise intensifies. He hears a familiar intro, but he can't place it."

" 'Coming Home for Keeps,' " she says. "He'll end up with 'Lovin' You.' "

"You seen the show before?"

She shakes her head. "Not this one. But they're all about the same. Save the biggest one for the last encore. I always figure that's how they guarantee the curtain calls, by holding out the big one."

"I guess that's just about the way it all works."

111

When Tommy has finished his last encore with "Lovin' You," Bad wanders over to the next dressing room. It is already packed. Cans of beer shoot up from the corner of the room like mortar shells into the crowd of people. He finds Tommy in the corner, changing his shirt.

"You're pissed because I cut in on your set."

"No," Bad says, "I'm not pissed at all. Thanks."

"You were welcome in mine. I would have appreciated it."

"I figured you had it covered. I had albums to sell."

"Goddamn it. Why are you busting my hump, Bad? What exactly is my fault here? What the hell do you want from me?"

"An album. Nothing more. I ain't asking for a damn thing. You did real well on the last one."

"I told you, you got the album. But you've got it when J.M.I. says they're ready for it. I can't do a damn thing about it."

"Then I don't want anything. Except to say thanks and good night."

"Damn it, Bad. I'm trying to be friends here. Stick around. Tomorrow's a rest day. We'll probably have a pretty good party here. There's booze, there's girls, somebody's got some pretty good blow around here. Get off your fucking high horse. Stick around and have some fun."

"I've got to drive tomorrow. I'm playing Utah tomorrow night. I believe I'll get my gear and go back to the hotel."

"Shit. Suit yourself. Ralphie's around here somewhere. Check with him. He'll take care of you."

"Right. Well, take care of yourself, Tommy."

"You, too, Bad. I'll be in touch on the album."

Bad starts to work his way through the jam of people. A couple slap him on the back and say, "Good show."

"Bad." Tommy is behind him, still shirtless. "Write me a couple of songs."

"Think you can walk through one without all the damn horns and strings?"

"I might manage."

"I'll see what I can do."

He is on his way out the back of the coliseum, carrying his guitar and amp, heading toward the parking lot.

"You packing it in for the night?" It is Linda, sitting on an amp crate, smoking a cigarette.

"I believe I've pretty well had it for tonight."

"You want some company?"

"You don't want to stick around for the big party?"

"They're all pretty predictable, too."

"Come on."

In the hotel room she lights a cigarette, takes one long drag, sets it in the ashtray and begins to undress. When she is naked, she takes up the cigarette, takes another drag, sets it back down, and steps up to and begins undressing him. When she has his clothes off, she gently pushes him back to the bed, sets him down and kneels down to his cock.

He runs his fingers down her neck and back, as far as he can reach, fingering the red marks left by her underwear. She raises her arms a little so he can get to her breasts. Her body is lean and young, her skin rich and smooth, nearly white where her bathing suit has blocked the sun. Her breasts are small and firm. It has been years since he has touched a body like this, unlined, unscarred, not dimpled with fat.

The smoothness of her skin makes him conscious of his own body, the sagging belly and hairy breasts, nearly as large as hers, the sweat chilling under the air-conditioning. Under the semicircles of her buttocks, he can see the bottoms of her feet, the pink toes, and next to them, his own, white as death, his toes twisted and callused from years of wearing cowboy boots. She is methodical, urging and coaxing him on, running her fingernails gently over the skin of his inner thighs.

He leans forward, trying to get his face into her red hair, but as he leans, his belly forces her head back, her teeth scraping him. She gently pushes him back. What, he wonders, does someone as young as this, with a body like this, want with someone like him?

Later, when she is asleep, the covers pulled up to her chin, her hair splayed over her face, he eases out of bed, lights a cigarette and moves to turn out the light. He stops to look at her. She is probably twenty-five, if she is that old. He can't remember how long it has been since he has held someone this young. He may never hold another. And beyond that, the other thought, that he misses Jean, scar, lines and fat. Given the choice, he guesses, he would trade.

113

Chapter Nine

He has four hours to kill before the show. He turns on the television. A thin man in a striped apron is pounding a piece of veal between pieces of plastic. "You want a larger portion? Just pound it longer." He turns off the television.

He sits down with his guitar. He begins chording through the standard progression in E, hoping he will find a note here that will lead him to something. "Home cooking," he thinks. There might be something there. He runs the scale a couple of times. Home cooking and home loving. Getting fat is like getting loved. He goes to the relative minor. There is something here, he is sure of it. He is also sure he doesn't have the patience to go through all the crap he is going to have to wade through to find it.

He puts down the guitar and picks up the telephone. It is not until the desk clerk answers that he knows exactly what he is going to do. "Long distance, please. Information."

"What city?" the operator asks.

"Santa Fe. New Mexico."

It never occurred to him to get her phone number, and now he realizes that it may be unlisted. By the time this has settled in, the operator is back on the line, giving him the number.

"Hello," a small voice says.

"Buddy, this is Bad, your old buddy."

"Buddy."

"Right. How are you doing, Buddy?"

"Watching Big Bird."

"How's Big Bird?"

"He talked to the policeman."

"That's good. Do you know the policeman is your friend?"

"Yeah."

"That's good, too. Is your mom there?"

"Yeah."

"Will you go get her so I can talk to her? Then you can go back and see what old Big Bird is up to."

The line goes dead for a few seconds, then Jean's voice.

"This is Bad."

"Bad?"

"Yeah. It's Bad. How are you?"

"Where are you?"

"Utah. Cedar City."

"What . . . ? I mean, I'm sorry, Bad. I didn't expect to hear from you. You caught me by surprise."

"Yeah, me too, as a matter of fact. I was thinking about you. I just decided to call."

"How was Phoenix? How was the show? And Tommy Sweet?"

"It was O.K. It was a show. It was nothing special."

"You and Tommy get along all right?"

"We had some drinks, talked. We're going to do an album, but I don't know when."

"That's nice."

"I've been thinking about you lately."

"Lately? It's only been a couple of days."

"Yeah, but damned funny thing, it seems long, I mean since I saw you. I've been thinking of you since."

"It was nice."

"You think any about me?"

"A lot. I've been finishing the article."

118

"That's not what I meant."

"I know. I'm sorry. Yes. I've thought about you. I had a good time."

"Listen. I get off the road in another week. Then I have four days before I go back to Houston. I want to stop off in Santa Fe. I want to see you."

She pauses for a long time. "You could do that."

"Hell. You're not making this easy. You want me to stop by or not? You don't want me to, I won't."

She pauses again. "Yes. Yes, I guess I want you to."

"I guess I'll be stopping by in about eight days, then. On the ninth. I think I can be there by early evening."

"The ninth?"

"That's a Friday."

"Friday. That's good."

"Maybe we could take Buddy to the zoo or something. Is there a zoo in Santa Fe?"

"I'll look forward to it. We both will."

"Me, too. So I'll see you next Friday."

"I miss you."

When she has hung up the phone, he holds on to it for a moment. Say that once more, he whispers.

There are still a couple of hours until he has to get ready. He pulls on his boots and a shirt, and heads across the street to the bar. It is still fairly early in the afternoon, and the bar is quiet.

Bad walks to the back of the bar to check out the action at the pool table. There are three guys, two playing, one watching. They are playing straight eight ball, and they are playing respectably, calling their shots, making enough of them. The man in the plaid shirt is obviously the better of the two. He has a steady hand, and as Bad watches, he sees that he has enough knowledge of the game that he is setting up shots in advance and moving the game quickly. Bad walks over to the table and places a quarter on the rail, then goes through the rack until he finds a twenty-three-ounce cue that is pretty straight, not too worn at the tip. When the game is finished, he picks up his quarter, runs it and racks.

"We can play for drinks if you want," Plaid Shirt tells him. "Or not, it doesn't matter. But that's as high as we go here. It's a friendly game."

"That suits me just fine."

Plaid Shirt breaks and takes down three stripes before he misses.

When he does, he doesn't leave much. Bad takes out his glasses, surveys the table and takes the hardest shot, working for position. "Three ball, off the cushion." The cue ball comes off the cushion slowly and nudges the three ball into the corner pocket, easing behind the twelve. The shot leaves him a straight shot at the six. He hits it low for backspin so the cue ball stops dead on impact, leaving him a line to the far end of the table. He sinks the four and the seven before he misses the one on a side carom.

Plaid Shirt takes two more before he misses. This time he mishits and leaves Bad a clear table. He runs it.

"Nice shooting," Plaid Shirt says. "What are you drinking?" Bad looks around at what the others are drinking. "One of those drafts will be just fine."

He takes the other two players easily. He hasn't played on the road, but at home he plays for five or six hours a week. When Plaid Shirt brings his beer, he sips at it, playing conservatively but pulling away from the others easily. He begins taking harder shots than necessary, just trying to play against himself since neither of these guys is providing any competition. When Plaid Shirt is up again, he gives Bad a tight smile and puts his quarter into the slot. "Is this going to hurt again?" he asks.

Bad smiles and breaks. He likes the sound of that. "Is this going to hurt again?" He could do something with that.

"Mr. Blake," Brenda says, "hold for Mr. Greene."

Suddenly the earpiece of the telephone oozes recorded music. Ten million strings play Dolly Parton. The business has gone to the dogs.

"Bad, how're you doing?"

"I'm not going to play another date, Jack. I'm off tomorrow night and that's it. No more, damn it. No more."

"Bad. Bad. No more. No problem, you're done after tomorrow night. I'm not going to overbook you. I want you to get some rest."

"Jack, if you found out your sister was turning five-dollar tricks, you'd overbook her."

"Cute, Bad. Remind me, next time I'll put you in a couple of comedy clubs."

"Might as well, the clown bands you've stuck me with."

"You ever tried to book bands in New Mexico?"

"New Mexico you did O.K. It was all the rest you fucked up."

"That's the first time you've ever admitted I did anything right. You're slipping, Bad."

"No. It's the first time you did anything right."

"Hell. That means I'm slipping. Anyway, I've got some news from Tommy. Apparently you actually did yourself some good for a change."

"Yeah, I refused to whip his ass at golf."

"Whatever you did, you did well. I got a check for twenty-five hundred for the albums you sold."

"You cocksucker."

"I know, Brenda told me."

"Bless her heart."

"Ditto. And I have a contract here, offering you a five-thousand-dollar advance for an album to be recorded at a future date, to be specified by the end of this calendar year. Plus another two thousand for first refusal rights to all songs written or co-written by you over the next two years."

"Holy shit."

"Ditto."

"I'll sign for the album but not the songs."

"It's the same contract."

"X out the song part, and I'll sign."

"I don't think we can do that."

"Hell, you're a lawyer; of course we can do that."

"I mean, I think they did it this way to make it a package deal, take it or leave it."

"I'll leave it."

"The hell you'll leave it."

"I don't write songs, Jack."

"Of course you write songs. Almost half of your income over the last ten years has been off songs you wrote."

"Wrote, Jack, wrote. I don't write songs."

"According to this contract, you don't have to. All they are asking is first refusal rights."

"No dice. If I write another song, it's my song, not Tommy's."

"Bad, you don't have a label anymore. If you write a song, how are you going to record it?"

"I don't give a good goddamn whether I record it or not. If it's my song, it's my song. I'm not going to work for Tommy Sweet."

"All he's asking is the right to see everything you write. It doesn't mean everything you write belongs to him. This is first right of refusal, not indentured servitude."

121

"I don't have dentures. They're my own teeth, they're my own songs."

"This is seventy-five hundred dollars. I believe you could use that kind of money."

"I'm working on a song, Jack. I want it for myself."

"So we'll negotiate it with Tommy. I'm sending the contract to Houston. Sign it."

"You sign it. You've got power of attorney. At least sign the damn thing for me."

"Right. Think about this, Bad. Tommy has just kicked in nine grand in the last two weeks. Maybe you could ease up on him."

"He's a bastard with a nice checkbook."

"Have it your way, but this is now your best year in the last seven. Brenda has some messages for you. Get some rest and I'll talk to you when you're back home."

"Right."

There is a pause, a couple more bars of market music, then Brenda's voice. "Mr. Blake. You've had a few phone calls. Let me give you the numbers."

"Did you really give Jack my message?"

She laughs, "It was a bad day. I gave it to him word for word."

"You sweet thing."

"It was my pleasure. You ready for these numbers? Terry in Houston wants you to call him right away, he says you have his number."

"Right."

"Then there is a message from a Mr. Wilks in Dallas; his number is—"

"I don't know Mr. Wilks. Who is he?"

"I don't know; he just wants you to call."

"It's somebody who wants something, an interview or to listen to his new song. Can it."

"You've got it. You have a good trip home."

"I believe I will. I do believe I will. Wait, Brenda, hold on a second. What's a nice perfume?"

"For who?"

"For a woman. What would you want someone to give you?"

"Serious or just fooling around?"

"Maybe serious."

"I like Opium. It's expensive, though."

"That's O.K. Tell Jack to wire me some money this afternoon."

The perfume is the easy part. That only takes a good portion of his cash. By his reckoning, it would cost about five hundred to get even the beginnings of a buzz off it. The hard part happens in the toy store. He has not been in a toy store in over twenty years. The last time he was in one, it was small and filled with dolls, cap guns, balls and bats, games and stuffed toys. This one has all of those plus computers, tape recorders and stuff he can't even recognize. The salesman points out the favorite toys: Gobots, Transformers, He-Man, G.I. Joe, Star Wars or Rambo. What it all comes down to, no matter how many guns, knives, bows and arrows, or muscles, is dolls. He considers a plastic guitar, but toy instruments seem wrong to him. He ends up with a riding fire engine and a foam basketball with a hoop that hangs over a closet door.

When he has finished the final set, shaken hands with the people who have stayed for last call, packed up his equipment and said goodbye to the band, he is tempted to get in the van and head out of Utah. He has about six hundred and fifty miles to drive. If he left now, he would end up in Santa Fe about two o'clock in the afternoon. He has told her early evening. He goes back to the motel and leaves a wake-up call for five o'clock. That will give him a little over three hours of sleep.

By noon he knows he has chosen the worst route. He has driven more vertical miles than horizontal. As soon as he hits a stretch of straight level road, the brush at the roadside grows coarse and dense. The van starts to knock in third, and he is climbing again. He tries to calculate the hours it will take to drive another three hundred miles in second gear.

He is weary of scenery, and his legs are starting to cramp. In the last six weeks he has driven three thousand miles, most of it on three or four hours' sleep. He drives straight through, stopping only for gas and coffee. Food he buys at drive-ins where he does not have to get out of the van or even stop the engine.

Near the New Mexico border he stops for gas in a small station and gets the mileage to Santa Fe. Inside the station, a mongrel dog, part shepherd, raises his head and wags his tail. "Nice dog," Bad says to the guy who is charging his gas.

"Damn good dog," the guy says. "He might not look like much, but he's a goddamn killer. He likes you. Course, you're white. Let a goddamn nigger or Indian come in, and you'd better believe it's a different story."

The dog wags his tail. The guy comes around the counter and takes a swiping kick at the dog, who jumps back and bares his fangs. "You was a nigger, he'd tear your throat out. That's a good dog. He hates niggers and Indians."

The dog is backed into the corner of the wall and counter, his fangs still bared, watching the owner. "I don't know about that," Bad says. "Looks like a good judge of character to me."

"He hates niggers. I got him for my wife. A damn nigger comes around her, that dog'll kill him."

"Must be a big disappointment to your wife."

"Yeah. What? Hell no. My old woman's a good woman. She hates niggers and Indians."

"If she is a good woman, I'd get me a pack of those dogs if I was you."

"Hey, what the hell are you sayin'? You sayin' my old woman's got a taste for niggers? That what you're sayin'? You get back here."

As he climbs into the van, the dog follows him out. "You poor son-of-a-bitch," Bad says.

As he drives, images from a dream come back to him, a dream that never got finished but was cut off by the wake-up call. He is in a small bar, not one he has played before but one that might be all the bars he has played before. He cannot quiet the crowd, who keep getting up from their seats, heading for the door and coming back in again. He has this new song, and he is going to sing it for them, but only if they won't tell anybody what it is. If he can get them to stay in their seats, Tommy won't find out about it. "You have to be real quiet now," he tells them. Half of them get up from their seats and head for the door, where Tommy is waiting. He keeps tuning the guitar and trying to hold the song in. Before he can sing it for them, the phone rings.

The song he was about to sing is called "Is This Going to Hurt Again?" As he drives, he works with the one line, trying others with it. That line is a chorus, he figures. He tries it as a first line, putting it to the melody of the fragment he came up with between Colorado and New Mexico: "Is this going to hurt again? / I can't take any more / Long, lonely nights, walking the floor." Then he tries: "I can't take any more / Of saying goodbye, and slamming the door." And other fragments: "I think about love every now and then / But then I stop and ask myself / Is this going to hurt again?"

What he needs is a guitar. If he could hear the music, test the possibilities on the guitar, he could find his way through this. Once he has a line or two, the phrasing of the music always suggests the rest of the lines. Trying to sing the song and invent the words at the same time is like trying to paint a wall as you're building it. He has always believed that he never wrote songs anyway, he just copied down songs that already existed somewhere in his mind.

He has the feeling that if he stopped, he could do most of the song in about a half hour. But it is nearly sundown and he's still a hundred and fifty miles or so from Santa Fe. The light is failing, he is sleepy and his back is beginning to stiffen on him. He keeps shifting position to try to put the pressure on different muscles. If he shifts to his right and pushes forward on the seat, he can stretch the cramping muscles, but he keeps slipping back. Finally, he hooks his left foot under the brace of the seat and lets the angle of his leg hold him in the position he wants.

He keeps working those phrases again, trying to hear the melody, the phrases that move it from verse to chorus in the attempt to work backward into the song. From what he knows, he tries to build an intro. A quick run from E to A to B⁷ and backward through A to E. He tries tuning the guitar, hearing the notes and running a quick E scale. "You'll have to be real quiet," he tells them. "I can't sing this song unless you're real quiet, stay in your seats and promise not to tell anyone what I have done." But they don't stay quiet and they don't stay in their seats. He keeps tuning, but they won't settle down. He keeps looking toward the door.

He hears the crunch of the tires on gravel and then an easy thump. He sees grass and brush and a wire fence coming at him in slow motion. He moves his foot to the brake and turns the wheel, but he is moving in slow motion, too, and the van is bouncing across the scrub brush at the side of the road, rocking slowly from side to side, over the fence. He hears the wire of the fence scraping the side of the van and pulling brush with it until the tree is in front of him. He turns the wheel as hard as he can, but the impact sends him across the wheel and into the windshield.

For a minute, he does not know where he is or why he is sitting here. His head is cold and his hand hurts. He sees his hat on the floor next to him in a pile of sheet music and a Styrofoam hamburger box. Around him, everything is wet and sticky. He bends over to pull his hat away from the mess of paper and spilled Coke, and pain blooms in front of his eyes like a Chinese firecracker. Things spin and the world implodes.

When he comes to again, his leg feels like it is strung with hot wires from ankle to hip. He tries to move it, and pain sends hamburger and bile burning up his throat. He eases himself back upright. Now his head is beginning to throb. He checks his face in the rearview mirror. He has a bump and a small cut across the top of his forehead. There is a thin trickle of blood in a winding stream down to his eyebrow.

What worries him is his leg. He can see that his foot is still hooked behind the seat brace. He tenderly runs his hands down the calf of his leg, over the tops of his boot until they reach his ankle. Slowly, gently, he pulls at the ankle to free his foot. A wave of cold splashes up from inside him and the inside of the van darkens to black.

"You O.K.?"

There is a hand on his shoulder, and a face at the window of the van.

"You O.K.?"

Bad leans his head back against the top of the seat and slowly nods his head. "Yeah, I'm O.K. Accident. Fell asleep."

"Can you get out?" The man opens the door of the van slowly, holding on to Bad's shoulder with his other hand.

"My leg. I think I broke my leg."

"Try to get out. Grab on to me."

The man, Bad is aware, is much smaller than he is, but when the door is open and he has turned around in the seat so he is facing the door, the man's hands grip him hard under the arms and lift him from the seat. Bad reaches out, and puts his arm around the man's shoulder. They do a slow, intricate waltz out of the van, lean up against it, and then spin heavily across the grass to where a pickup truck idles, its taillights flashing red.

"It doesn't look too bad," the man says when he comes back to the truck. "Crunched your right fender, busted a headlight. You got a flat tire. Not too bad. And you got about twenty yards of fence, too." He hands Bad the keys. "I locked it." He starts the truck.

Bad hears the crunch of gravel under the tires as the truck noses out onto the road. "Wait," he says. "Wait. My guitar."

126

When the man comes back with the guitar, Bad remembers. "Fire truck, get the fire truck, too."

"Ain't no fire, buddy. It's all O.K."

He wants to explain about Buddy's fire truck, to go back and get it, but he feels too tired to speak.

He rides huddled against the door, shivering, trying not to move. His ankle has begun to throb. The man keeps poking him in the shoulder.

"You got a bump on your head. You might have a concussion. I don't think you should sleep. Talk to me. You a musician?"

"Yeah."

"What kind?"

"Guitar."

"I know that. Come on, talk to me. What kind of music do you play?"

"Country."

"Yeah? You know Kenny Rogers? I really like him. You know 'Lucille'? Come on, sing it with me."

"My ankle," Bad says.

" 'You picked a fine time to leave me, Lucille,' " the man croaks. "Come on, 'With four hungry kids and a crop in the field.' Come on, you know it."

Bad tries to mumble a harmony behind him.

The hospital is light and full of angles that spin past him. Every time he looks up, lights shine in his eyes. He closes them tight and Tommy is there with golf clubs, asking him if he wants a drink. He reaches for the bottle and Tommy pulls it away and laughs a sharp, brittle laugh. As Tommy laughs, he runs his hands through his hair, drawing his ears out to long red points. He runs a hand across his face and pulls it sharp and covered with red fur. His nose is small and black above the long red whiskers. His tongue lolls over the rows of small white pointed teeth. The yellow eyes shine and dart. His upper lip wrinkles and pulls up away from the little teeth. Tommy darts forward, sinking his teeth into Bad's ankle. Then he runs, skittering across the tile floor of the hospital and under the root of a tree and gone.

Chapter
Ten

When he wakes he is in bed, but he is not sure where. The vertical blinds, the bed rails, the curtain, slowly come into focus. He is in the hospital, he knows that. He has had an accident. There is someone in another bed, next to him.

"Where am I?" he asks.

"Hospital," the man answers. "You got a busted ankle. They brought you in late last night. You were gone, man."

"Where? Where are we?"

"Taos. That what you mean? You want a nurse? I can call one for you."

Nurses are in and out all morning. He is questioned and poked. He drifts in and out of dreamless sleep, waking to thermometers, needles to the inside of the elbow, and the puffing sleeve of the sphygmoma-nometer. "Where am I?" he keeps asking them. "The hospital," they assure him confidently.

When he remains awake, he checks the damage. There is a bandage

131

on his forehead and a plaster cast on his left ankle, about as long as
the shaft of a good boot. His neck, shoulders and back are all sore
and tight. He has pain, but more, he has questions: what is wrong with
him, where is he, where is his guitar, where is his van, and when can
he get out of here?

"I'll call the nurse again," the guy in the next bed says, "if you can
stay awake long enough to talk to her."

"Call," he says. His throat is parched and his lips are cracking.

"Simple fracture of the fibula," she tells him. "Broken ankle. A
minor concussion. You are in the hospital, Taos, New Mexico; your
guitar is in the closet with your clothes. About your van, you'll have
to contact the New Mexico Department of Public Safety, and when
you can leave is up to the doctor."

"Soon?" he asks.

"Probably."

"Today?"

"Probably not."

"Get me the doctor."

"If you can make it down the hall, you can call from the pay phone,
it's cheaper," the guy in the next bed advises.

Bad considers the white cocoon around his ankle and the pain that
seems to squeeze up out of it and spiral up his leg. He calls the DPS
from the phone beside the bed.

After he is forced to spell out his name, his whole name, his legal
name, over the phone, he is told his van is at the impound lot in Taos.
He needs proof of insurance, and two hundred sixty-eight dollars to
cover impound fees and forty yards of wire-mesh fence and six fence
posts, plus labor. He is also being cited for Failure to Control Vehicle.
He gives them Jack's phone number.

The doctor, the nurse tells him, will be in to see him before long.
In the meantime, she wants to know what kind of medication he is
taking for his blood pressure.

"None," he says. "An occasional whiskey. But only once in a
while."

"Terrific," she says. "Your blood pressure is one eighty-five over
ninety-five."

"That's not good, huh?"

"That's not real good."

132

"I could drink a couple more, I guess."

The problem, the doctor explains, is not really the ankle. It's a pretty clean break and should heal without undue complication, though at his age, who really knows? He will have to stay off it for at least six weeks, but he can leave in the morning. The problem, as the doctor sees it, is his general condition, or lack of condition. His blood pressure is way too high, his heart has a fairly pronounced arrhythmia, and there is considerable chest congestion. And from the responses he gave the nurse earlier in the morning, it is clear that his drinking and smoking have slipped to something beyond excess.

"I was still asleep then," Bad says. "I didn't know what I was saying. If I'd been awake, I would have lied. Then we'd both be happier."

The doctor is young and sweet-looking. He has short brown hair, a neatly trimmed beard and wire-rim glasses. He wears a western shirt and a bolo tie below the open collar. He wears corduroy jeans, and Bad knows that he wears rounded shoes with crepe soles. He is sincere, and sincerely trying to be kind. But Bad figures that anyone who is willing to stick two fingers up your ass and poke around like that enjoys his work. The pretense of kindness doesn't go very far.

The real problem, the doctor tells him, is not that he is going to die. That's not a problem, that's a simple fact. The real problem is that he probably is not going to die for quite a while yet. Bad does not consider this a serious problem.

"Let me explain it to you this way," the doctor begins. "If it was simply a matter of life expectancy, you might decide that it is worth the gamble. You go on living the way you are, the way you seem to think you want to live, and then in a couple of years, four or five angels lift you up into heaven with a lot of harp music in the background. That would be great. You've paid your money, you've taken your choice. You've traded ten or twenty years of your life for the right to live any damn way you choose. Good enough. The only thing is, it doesn't work that way. The kinds of stuff we're talking about here—emphysema, congestive heart failure, cancer, an extremely good chance of stroke—are more debilitating than quickly and cleanly fatal. They will kill you, there's no mistaking that, but they're going to do it slowly, painfully, and humiliatingly. You're going to end up helpless as a child, in all probability.

"Mr. Blake, are you going to talk to me?"

"About what?"

"Look, Mr. Blake, I have other patients to see. Obviously, you don't want to hear any of this. You've got a broken ankle, you want to go home. I understand that. But when I see something like this, I have to say something. You don't want to hear it, and I don't particularly want to say it, but I've got to. You come in here from an auto accident; after I set your ankle, I find a fifty-six-year-old man who is rapidly starting to wear out. You smoke two packs of unfiltered cigarettes a day; you are a good thirty pounds overweight; your blood pressure is way too high; you obviously get no exercise; you clearly eat anything at all; and let's not kid ourselves about this one: you're an alcoholic.

"What you want is to get rid of the pain in your ankle and get out of here, then you'll feel better. But don't you see you're not going to feel much better, even without the pain? I'm telling you: stop smoking, stop drinking, lose twenty-five pounds. You do that, you'll feel better. I can make recommendations for ways to do that. Your own doctor can help you. But that's what you've got to do. It's your choice, but you don't have any real options. In the meantime, stay off the leg."

"He didn't give you cholesterol and salt," the guy in the next bed says. "That comes next. Give up all that, and then it's cholesterol and salt. It's always something."

"I'd give up cholesterol and salt and kiss his ass for a drink," Bad says.

"Bad, where are you?" He tries to gauge the distance in her voice.

"Taos," he says.

"Taos? I waited up most of the night for you. I thought you were going to be here last night."

"I'm in the hospital."

"Oh, my God."

"I had an accident. I'm sorry. I broke my ankle. I wasn't drinking. I just had an accident."

"Are you O.K.?"

"Well, no. I broke my ankle."

"Oh jeez, I'm sorry."

"No, look. I'm sorry. I was about an hour and a half out of Santa Fe last night and I fell asleep. It was my own damn fault. And it's not all that bad. I get out of here in the morning."

"Are you still going to come here?"

134

"If I can. If it's all right with you."

"I'll come and get you."

"I can drive. My van's O.K. as far as I can tell."

"I'll come and get you. I'll take the bus in the morning."

"You really don't have to."

"I'm coming. I want to."

"That's wonderful."

He likes getting pushed down the hall in the wheelchair, his left leg stuck out in front like a cowcatcher. He is still in his gown, but he has his hat, stained at the brim from the spilled Coca-Cola. He nods and smiles to the people he passes. In 1963, he rode in the Rose Bowl Parade, two cars behind the grand marshal. This is oddly similar.

In the physical therapy room, he is held up by two orderlies, while he is measured and crutches are adjusted for him. The crutches are not as easy as they look. He keeps dropping down and catching his armpits on the braces. He is having trouble getting the rhythm of swinging the heavy cast ahead of him as he goes. He stops and sits on the therapy table. "Shit," he says. "This would be a hell of a lot easier if I had a drink."

"Walk ten times across the room," the therapist says.

"Hell, I can't walk that three times, much less ten."

"O.K.," the therapist says, "we'll send the chair back. You can walk back to your room with your butt hanging out. One way or another, you'll learn to use those."

Bad slides off the table and starts swinging himself across the room.

When she arrives, he has been sitting in the wheelchair for an hour and a half, ready to go. He has dressed in the clothes he was wearing when he had the accident. The left leg of his jeans is slit up to the knee. He has his guitar and left boot on his lap.

"I'll only stay a day or so, then I'll head back to Houston," he tells her in the taxi on the way to the impound yard. "You don't need some old gimp hanging around being a bother."

"Nonsense. You won't be a bother."

"If I'm as good at being laid up as I think I'm going to be, I'll be a hell of a bother."

*　　　*　　　*

The van is worse than he has expected. It's drivable, but the right front fender is smashed and there is a small crack at the lower corner of the windshield. The bumper is twisted on the right, and the grille is pushed in. The headlight is gone, and there are long scratches down both sides, where he has dragged the fence along with him. It looks like three or four hundred dollars' worth of damage.

The impound bill has been taken care of out of Jack's office. He has to sign release forms and a citation for Failure to Control Vehicle. He has a court date in two weeks to answer the charge.

"Can I just pay this?" he asks.

"Call the district court," the trooper tells him. "They'll take a plea over the phone and assess the fine. You better get that headlight fixed right away. The second you are off this lot, you are in violation. You could pick up another citation for Faulty Equipment."

"Jesus, Lord. You aren't going to pull that kind of shit on me, are you?"

"I'm here at this desk. I'm not going to cite anyone. I can't speak for anyone else, though. I'd get it fixed right away."

"Yeah. Damn. I'll get right to it." He swings away from the desk on his crutches, holding himself stiff with his forearms, careful of his already tender armpits. "I got a flat tire there. Anyone here to change it for me?"

"I'm sorry, sir, we're not staffed to take care of those items."

"I'll pay."

"Sorry, sir. No can do."

"I'll do it," Jean says. "Don't worry about it."

"Mr. Blake," the trooper calls, "it was nice to meet you. I've always liked your songs."

"Khaki bastard," he says to Jean when they are out the door.

"That was sort of nice. I mean, to say he likes your songs."

"My ex-wives all liked my songs, too. They tried to cut my heart out. There isn't anything as treacherous as a fan."

Jean jacks up the van and pulls the bad tire and wheel with little difficulty. Bad hobbles around her, looking for something to do. He keeps fluttering his hands and saying, "Hell, you shouldn't be doing this." She gets the spare, mounts it and runs the lug nuts tight.

"Is there anything you need?" she asks as she wheels the van into the street. "Did you have breakfast?"

"Yeah. I had something in the hospital."

"What did you have?"

"Food. That was as close as I could identify it. What time is it?"

"Quarter after eleven."

"Could we stop for a drink?"

"Isn't it a little early for that?"

"Depends on how you look at it. To me, it looks like about two days late."

"Can't you wait until we get to Santa Fe?"

He is trying to light a cigarette, his hand shaking so hard he has to brace it with the other. "I don't think so."

He is flat on his back in Jean's bed. His foot is propped up on two cushions from the sofa in the living room. Both of the pillows from the bed are behind his head. On the table beside him are his cigarettes and a bottle of Jack Daniel's. At the foot of the bed is the television, wheeled in from the living room. On the television, lives tangle and knot into ruin. He can hear Jean moving through the other rooms.

On the television, two women talk. One fights back tears. The other keeps talking, hesitates, then turns and leaves. In the hall, beyond the door, she stops. "She needs someone to talk to," she says to no one Bad can see. She moves back to the door. Talk, Bad thinks, is not what she needs. She's going to need someone to walk to. He repeats that. Then he throws back the covers and slips out of bed. He hops to the other side of the room, where his guitar is propped against the chair.

It comes as easily to him as an old song recalled after years, in E flat: "She's going to need someone to walk to, / When she walks out on you. / She's going to need someone to talk to, / When she finally says she's through." It slips like grease on a skillet from E flat to A flat, back to E flat and up to B flat.

He calls Jean in and sings it for her. "She's going to need someone to walk to, / And it's going to be me instead of you."

"You know that song?" he asks.

"I think so," she says. "I'm sure I've heard it."

"Yeah," he says, "that's the way it is. The good ones are the ones you're sure you've heard before. That's the next hit for Tommy Sweet."

"You wrote that?"

"Just now. Just fifteen minutes ago. I'm afraid that's going to be about all I'm going to be good for for a little while here."

137

"No," she says, slipping back the covers. "That's not why you're here."

"So how the hell did this happen?" Jack asks.

"I fell asleep. I'd been driving for fifteen hours."

"Drinking?"

"No. Goddamn it, no. I fell asleep."

"O.K., O.K. What are you doing in Santa Fe?"

"Visiting a friend."

"Friend?"

"A friend. People who aren't so goddamned suspicious have them."

"You have any idea how much your marriages have cost you over the years? You've spent more on alimony than some folks make in their whole lives."

"I ain't marrying anybody. I'm visiting my friend."

"When are you going to be back in Houston?"

"In a couple of days. Terry is auditioning new bass players. I'll be back in time to get started. It wouldn't go any faster with me there."

"O.K. Have Brenda give you the insurance policy number. Call the office and get them working on getting the van fixed. Can you drive?"

"Yeah. I can drive. I will drive. I'll be there by the first of the week."

"Take care of yourself, Bad."

"I wasn't drinking."

Jean comes into the room with two cups of coffee. "You want me to call him?"

"Why?"

"To tell him that I'm not about to marry you."

"You might have waited until I asked before you turned me down."

"Oh God, don't even joke."

"I'm not all that bad. They weren't all my fault. I think it was Kay Starr said, on the occasion of her fifth or sixth divorce, 'I guess it can't always be the guy's fault.' I've taken a lot of comfort from that."

"No, you're not bad at all, but I think you've missed the point there somehow."

"No. I just got a different one than she intended. I mean, it wasn't always my fault. I finally figured that one out. Most of them were, but not all of them."

She puts the coffee cups down and sits on the bed with him, pulling his head into her lap. "You worry about that a lot, don't you?"

"I got a twenty-four-year-old son. I haven't seen him since he was four. I don't know what he looks like. I don't know what he's doing. I don't know how he did in school. I don't know if he played baseball or had trouble with geography. I didn't see him ride his bike or teach him how to drive a car. I think about that a lot. That's my fault, that's all my fault, and that's a hell of a goddamned price to pay. It's a hell of a thing to be fifty-six years old and not know a damned thing about your own son."

"I couldn't live if I lost Buddy."

"That's the goddamnedest part. You do live."

"Why didn't you find them after they left?" They are sitting propped up in the bed, naked. He is smoking. She toys with sweated strands of hair at the back of his neck.

"I tried. I tracked her down to L.A. Even in L.A. she kept moving around. She knew I'd be following her. Then the record company got involved. They convinced me that I had to give up. I guess they were still thinking about Spade Cooley and all of that. Anyway, they told me it was either keep chasing them down or keep making records and money. Records and money seemed real important then."

"Who's Spade Cooley?"

"Spade Cooley was one of the best bandleaders in western swing. Maybe he was the best. All during the forties, he and Bob Wills were always about neck and neck. He wrote the song 'Shame on You.' It was really top-notch stuff. Anyway, in about nineteen sixty, sixty-one, he got the idea that his wife was cheating on him. That she was having an affair with Roy Rogers, as a matter of fact. So he killed her. Only it was worse than that. He got his little girl out of bed and took her into the living room and told her he was going to stomp her mother to death, and she was going to watch. Then he did it. He stomped her to death.

"It made the guys in the suits real nervous. I mean, this was a guy who was like you or me, and suddenly he snaps and beats his wife to death. So when they found out they had a two-hundred-and-twenty-pound drunk running around L.A., looking for the wife that had run out on him, they got pretty worried. They sent three guys after me. I woke up in a sanitarium, where they were supposed to be drying me out. First two days, I was in a straitjacket; after that, every time I woke up I took another needle in the ass. I didn't wake up for days."

"They locked you up?"

139

"It's true. I was worth a lot of money to them. Things were a lot different then. I mean, we all know about George Jones and his drinking, and people love it. But back then, they wouldn't let anything like that get out. I mean, when Hank Williams died, they got the official death certificate to read 'heart attack.' We all knew what killed him, but they didn't let stuff like that out.

"So Marge got smart. When she took off, she went to L.A. and went right to the boys in the suits. She convinced them that I was going to kill or at least beat her when I got to L.A. She let them know that if they didn't want another Spade Cooley on their hands, they better protect her from me. And the sort of reputation I had been building up went a long way to back her story.

"When they finally let me out, they gave me the word. I got the hell out of L.A. and didn't cause any more trouble, or I was back in the ward again. I don't scare real easy, but that scared the piss out of me. Those boys knew where the button was and how to push it.

"Anyway, I lost track of Marge and Steve. I got the divorce papers from the record company. By the time things had loosened up, it was all too late. I guess they're still in L.A., but I don't know."

"You could probably find them. I mean, if you looked."

"What the hell am I going to say? 'Hi, how you doing? What's been going on the last twenty years?' No. They don't need to see me now. They were better off without me, and I guess they still are. Marge was a good woman with a good head on her shoulders. They did all right. I'm sure of that."

"You could find them for your sake. Don't you think they owe something to you?"

"No. She was right. Marge was right to do what she did. I was a rotten father and a worse husband. They really were better off without me. Maybe that's what I would tell her, that she was right."

"No. I don't think so. I think you deserve better."

"I didn't. I'm not sure I do now, but I know I didn't then. There was the drinking, and there were pills, too. And I was on the road all the time. I mean, I couldn't stand being home for very long. There were no lights, no one applauded. That was out on the road, that and lots of women, lots of good times. I just figured that was all mine, I mean I had it coming, and a wife and a baby shouldn't change what was rightfully mine, and goddamn it, I didn't let it."

"Look. I won't even pretend I understand how someone could let a child go. And I think you owe it to both of you to try to find him again. Don't let what you've done stop you from being what you are."

"Most of my life anyway, that's been being a son-of-a-bitch."

"Well, I like you. I won't marry you, but I like you."

"If there's one thing in the world better than a pretty girl, it's a pretty girl who's gullible."

"If there's one thing better than a good man, it's a good man who's too crippled up to get away," she says, nestling up against him.

"You're welcome to break the other ankle."

In the morning, he is up before she is. The road has changed his rhythms. He wakes ready to get into the van and drive on to the next stop. He tries to be quiet, but as he swings his legs out of the bed, the cast on his left ankle clunks heavily on the floor. He bites his lip against the pain. Jean stirs but doesn't wake.

His crutches are across the room, leaning against the dresser. He stands, weight on his right leg. Slowly, he shifts it to his left. He is able to transfer only part of it before the pain flashes up from the ankle to the pit of his stomach. He shifts back to the right leg. He tries to calculate the furniture's strength to see if he can move from piece to piece across the room. Most of it is wicker. He sinks to his knees and crawls across the floor on hands and knees.

When he reaches the dresser, he gets the crutches and moves the five feet to the wicker hamper where she has draped his pants. He gets the left leg on, snaking the pants over the cast. Then he realizes that to get the right leg on, he will have to rest his weight on his left leg. He maneuvers back to the hamper and tests it with his weight. It seems sturdy enough. By sitting gingerly on it, he can work his right foot into the pants leg and start working the pants on. When he pulls them up, though, the cuff is still caught under his foot. He shifts his weight to the center of the hamper and lifts up his foot. When his foot clears the floor, his weight shifts backward, the top of the hamper gives and he goes in, butt first.

"Jesus," Jean screams, sitting suddenly upright. Then, "Oh, my God, Bad, are you all right?"

He is on the floor, his left leg up, sticking out of the broken hamper, his right leg splayed out and resting on top of an aralia palm in a ceramic pot. His pants are caught around his knees.

"Tell me you're all right," Jean says. "Please God, tell me you're all right."

"Help me up," Bad says. "I'm goddamned all right. Help me up."

"Thank God you're all right," she says, " 'cause I'm going to bust something if I can't laugh. That's the funniest goddamned thing I've ever seen. Where's my camera?"

"Help me up, goddamn it."

Bad is trying to get out of the smashed hamper, and Jean is rolling in the bed, when Buddy walks in. He watches wide-eyed as Jean pulls the sheets up and Bad tries to wiggle his jeans up to his hips. He walks over to where Bad is on the floor and pulls the palm plant off Bad's foot. "Can we have pancakes?" he asks.

In the kitchen, Bad gives orders and Buddy fetches for him. "You like apples?" Bad asks. Yes, Buddy nods. "Get some apples, then. I'm going to teach you the right way to cook. Let's see, you're four?" Yes, Buddy nods. "You married yet?" No. "Then you better learn how to cook. You know how to cook, you don't have to live with some mean old witch just because she keeps you fed."

Bad peels, cores and slices apples, then dices them and sets them aside. He sends Buddy to the refrigerator for milk and eggs, to the cupboard for flour, oil and a skillet. He sets Buddy on the counter and mixes the batter, explaining every step. When he has beaten the batter smooth, he adds the diced apples. When he drops the batter into the hot skillet, he shows Buddy how to wait until bubbles form, first at the edges, then in the center, before flipping the pancakes.

"I've got to go down to the paper for a while this morning," Jean says at breakfast. "I'll drop Buddy off at the day care center. You want me to take you somewhere, or do you want to stay here?"

"I don't know what I could do with this ankle. I'm not much for libraries and museums. Why don't you leave Buddy here with me?"

"You don't want to baby-sit. Besides, Buddy will want to see his friends today."

"I want to stay here," Buddy says.

"There you go. We want to stay here."

"And do what?"

"Man stuff," Bad says.

"Man stuff," Buddy says.

"You play cards?" Bad asks when Jean is gone.

"No."

"You know any good fishing stories?"

"No."

"Then maybe we ought to go take a walk and see what kind of trouble we can get into."

"Yeah."

He has difficulty negotiating the steps down from Jean's apartment to the sidewalk, but by stopping often and leaning his weight on the railing, he learns how to work the heavy cast gently from step to step.

The apartment complex is made up of several two-story buildings, each containing eight apartments. To avoid a look of monotonous conformity, they have been set at oblique angles to each other. The sidewalk that connects them curves and angles off around buildings and landscaping. Buddy runs ahead, out of Bad's sight, and then comes running back when Bad doesn't catch up. They have been walking only about five minutes. Bad does not know exactly where they are, but Buddy keeps leading him on.

Finally, Bad turns a corner and finds himself in the playground. There are swings, teeter-totters, and lots of telephone poles cut in odd lengths and sunk into the ground. Bad can handle the swing, braced on his crutches and pushing Buddy with one hand, and he can, awkwardly, do much the same to keep Buddy going on the teeter-totter. What Buddy really wants to do is play on the telephone poles. Bad has a rush of panic. They look dangerous, full of sharp edges and splinters. Why the hell do they give kids such artsy-fartsy stuff, stuff that could bust their heads open in a second? He has visions of Buddy's small body bent and crumpled at the bottom of the log pile, smeared with blood. How could any creature be as delicate and fragile as a child? He thinks back to what he played on as a kid. Rocks, trees and farm machinery, vines, a creek and a wooden footbridge over the creek—a miracle that any of them lived through it.

When Buddy is through with the telephone poles, he pulls Bad over to the swimming pool.

"The concrete pond," Bad tells him. There are two women next to it, in bathing suits. "It's a concrete pond, and they've got the thing stocked."

While Buddy runs around the fence surrounding the pool, Bad chats with one of the women. She is young and friendly, and her skin glitters with drops of sweat. He tells her about his accident, about the tour. She tells him she is a student at the university, studying business administration. He watches a drop of sweat run from her collarbone, around the curve of her breast and under her swimsuit top. Become a booking agent, he tells her; there is a fortune to be made off other people's work. When Buddy wearies of running the fence, he comes back to Bad and they head for the apartment.

"Take good care of your grandpa," the girl says.

*   *   *

"Turn on the sound," Buddy says.

"No," Bad says, "it's better to watch it this way. We can make up our own story."

"She's bad," Buddy says of the woman in the red dress.

"How do you know that, Bud?"

"I can tell. She's a bad lady. She has funny eyes."

"I wish I could figure it out that easy. O.K. She's a bad lady. What are we going to do about her?"

"Shoot her," Buddy says.

"No. You can't do that. That's the code of the West. You can't shoot a lady. What should we do?"

"You tell."

"I suppose, if it was me, I'd marry her."

Buddy puts his hands over his face and begins to giggle.

"That would fix her little red wagon, right?"

"You're silly."

"I guess you got that right, little buddy."

"You didn't even put him down for a nap?" Jean asks later that evening. "Even the day care center makes him take naps."

"We were having a good time. If I made him take a nap, what would I have done? Who would I have played with?"

"He really likes you. It's amazing."

"It's not. I'm a good guy. He knows that. Kids can tell."

She curls into him on the sofa. On the television, Shane has traded in his guns to be a peaceful farmhand for Jean Arthur and Van Heflin. "That's bullshit," Jean says. "Maybe it's right bullshit this time, but it's still bullshit."

"What are you going to do?"

"When?"

"Anytime. From now on. What are you going to do from now on?"

"Write. It's what I do. I'm going to keep on doing it. What are you going to do?"

• "There's only one thing I can do. But you've got a boy."

"That's right. And I'm doing O.K. He look underfed to you? Look, I ended up at thirty-four divorced and alone. I started writing, and I took care of myself writing. Then Buddy came along, and now I take care of both of us. I guess I can keep it up. Buddy and I are doing all right. There will be better jobs, better papers, magazines."

144